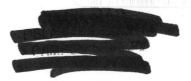

The Modern Language Association of America

Index Society Fund Publications

Carleton Brown and Rossell Hope Robbins. *The Index of Middle English Verse.* 1943.

Ralph W. Baldner. *Bibliography of Seventeenth-Century French Prose Fiction.* 1967.

Margaret Crum. *First-Line Index of English Poetry, 1500–1800, in Manuscripts of the Bodleian Library, Oxford.* 1969.

Donald Wing. *Short-Title Catalogue of Books Printed in England, Scotland, Ireland, Wales, and British America and of English Books Printed in Other Countries, 1641–1700.* Vol. 1, 1972. Vol. 2, edited by Timothy J. Crist, 1982.

J. Don Vann. *Victorian Novels in Serial.* 1985.

Victorian Novels
in Serial

J. Don Vann

*Publication of this book
has been supported by
the Index Society Fund of
the Modern Language Association of America*

The Modern Language Association of America
New York   1985

© 1985 by The Modern Language Association of America
All rights reserved. Printed in the United States of America

Library of Congress Cataloging-in-Publication Data

Vann, J. Don (Jerry Don), 1938–
   Victorian novels in serial.
   (Index Society Fund publications)
   Bibliography: p.
   1. English fiction—19th century—Bibliography.
   2. Serialized fiction—Great Britain—Bibliography.
   3. English periodicals—Bibliography.   I. Title.
   II. Series.
Z2014.F4V36   1985   [PR871]   016.823'8   84-20538
ISBN 0-87352-135-8

Second printing 1994

Published by The Modern Language Association of America
10 Astor Place, New York, New York 10003-6981

Printed on recycled paper

Contents

Preface   ix

Introduction   1

Contents

Robert Louis Stevenson 127

William Makepeace Thackeray 133

Anthony Trollope 141

Mrs. Humphry Ward 170

Notes on Periodicals 173

Selected Bibliography 177

Preface

This book is intended to serve two purposes: (1) to give a general introduction to serialization in the Victorian novel by providing a brief history, a sampling of novelists' comments on the mode of publication, and a discussion of its impact on the novel and (2) to identify that part of a novel which was included in each serial installment. The second purpose is by far the more important. The novels of authors such as Dickens, Trollope, and Thackeray in part issue and the magazines and newspapers containing the serials of Victorian novels are difficult to procure: when they are on the market, they are usually beyond scholars' budgets, and because libraries will rarely lend such items, scholars must find funds to travel to research libraries. This problem is compounded by the lack of adequate bibliographies of serialization for most Victorian novelists. For example, the content and dates of the installments of Ainsworth's *Old Saint Paul's* in the *Sunday Times* are not identified anywhere. Until this information was supplied by the present volume, one could have found it only by traveling to the British Library Newspaper Library at Colindale (the *Sunday Times* has not been published on microfilm yet). Some bibliographies, such as R. L. Purdy's *Thomas Hardy: A Bibliographical Study* (London: Oxford Univ. Press, 1954), do indicate the chapter numbers of serial parts, but none indicate the exact content when installment endings fall in the middle of a chapter. Only a few modern editions, notably the Penguin and Norton, identify serial endings.

Knowing where the serial installment began and ended allows modern readers to duplicate the reading experience of their nineteenth-century counterparts. When we begin to peruse *The Newcomes* in book form, for example, we fail to realize that in 1853 the reader received only three chapters each month. Criticizing a novel without taking into account the possible influence of serialization on structure and characterization may give us a distorted view.

In addition, this work allows the researcher to know the exact date on which specific parts of the text were available to Victorian readers. For this reason I have provided synopses of the American serials when the serial was published only in the United States or when the American version preceded the English. American serials that appeared later are cited but not synopsized. I have supplied the publication date of the volume edition whenever I was able.

The novelists covered in this volume are those included in *Victorian Fiction: A Guide to Research*, ed. Lionel Stevenson (1964; rpt. New York: MLA, 1980), and *Victorian Fiction: A Second Guide to Research*, ed. George Ford (New York: MLA, 1978), with the addition of William Harrison Ainsworth and Frederick Marryat. The following novelists are excluded because they never published in serial: the Brontës, Benjamin Disraeli, George Gissing, Samuel Butler, and George Moore. The selected bibliography cites studies of serialization.

The author gratefully acknowledges the following institutions for the use of their facilities: the British Library at Bloomsbury and the Newspaper Library at Colindale, the London Library, the Newberry Library, the Berg Collection of the New York Public Library, the Humanities Research Center of the University of Texas at Austin, and the North Texas State University Library. Also I must thank the libraries that were willing to lend materials and Ellie Whitmore of the Interlibrary Loan Department at North Texas State University for her valiant efforts in borrowing some scarce items. The following individuals generously gave their assistance and advice: Walter Achtert, director of research programs, Modern Language Association of America; Robert Colby, Queens College, City University of New York; Lionel Madden, College of Librarianship, Aberystwyth, Wales; Joanne Shattock and Philip Collins, University of Leicester; and Rosemary VanArsdel, University of Puget Sound. And my profound thanks go to the American Philosophical Society and the North Texas State University Faculty Research Fund Committee for their financial support. Finally, I want to thank my wife, Dolores, and my children for their encouragement and endurance.

Introduction

The History of Serialization

Serialization of Victorian novels took two forms: publication in installments in newspapers and magazines and publication in discrete installments—generally referred to as part issue or publication in numbers—that sometimes contained advertisements. Both practices had been used long before the nineteenth century, the first serialized work of fiction appearing perhaps as early as 1698, but their histories differ considerably.[1] In England, serial reprinting of novels in newspapers gained impetus after the Stamp Act of 1712, which required that half-sheet newspapers be printed on paper impressed with a halfpenny tax stamp and that full-sheet newspapers be on paper with a penny stamp.[2] Enterprising printers quickly found a loophole in this law, for the Stamp Act stated that publications larger than one whole sheet and less than book length should be classed as pamphlets. The tax rate for the entire run was only two shillings for each sheet of copy, a negligible sum. Many publishers began publishing newspapers composed of a sheet and a half, calling them pamphlets for tax purposes and printing them on unstamped paper. Running short of news stories, these publishers sometimes reprinted parts of novels in order to have enough material to fill one-and-one-half sheets.

Parliament, finally recognizing that revenue was being lost, revised the Stamp Act in 1724. Beginning 25 April 1725, newspapers printed on one-and-one-half sheets were no longer regarded as pamphlets but were printed on paper taxed at the rate of a penny per sheet. Under the revised law, publishers had no reason to reprint novels as filler. The reading public, however, had developed a taste for serial fiction, and, in fact, the practice of printing installments in newspapers increased after 1775.[3] Henceforth publishers used serialization as a means of maintaining their readership.

Of the Victorian novels included in the present study, however, the majority were published in magazines, a mode of publication that had been used throughout the eighteenth century.[4] The pioneer among Victorian novelists was Frederick Marryat, who had already published six novels in magazines by the time Victoria came to the throne. The serialization of novels in periodicals remained popular throughout the century.

Part issue had a different history. It began with Joseph Moxon's *Mechanik Exercises; or, The Doctrine of Handy-Works* in 1678, a manual sold in numbered monthly parts for consumers who probably could not manage to buy a volume but could afford the work in part issue. Over the next fifty years, some forty books were published in parts, most of them histories, geographies, and translations.[5] By 1733 the practice was firmly established.[6] Lawrence Sterne's occasional volume of *Tristram Shandy* was, in a sense, part issue of fiction. The eighteenth-century *Cheap Repository Tracts* by Hannah More and others may be viewed as the foundation of monthly part issue of original fiction in England.[7]

Readers in the early nineteenth century were used to seeing novels reissued in numbers, a practice made popular in the eighteenth century by the publisher Richard Bentley, but it was Dickens' first novel that established the popularity of part issue for the original publication of a novel. In March 1836 the publishers Chapman and Hall issued the first serial part of the *Pickwick Papers*. Through the first three months the project was uncertain, with each part selling only a few hundred copies, but with part 4 sales soared, eventually reaching forty thousand a month.[8]

The Effects of Serialization on Authorship

For almost forty years after the appearance of *Pickwick*, publishing in numbers was in vogue. It greatly enlarged the reading audience, who, like their counterparts buying Moxon's book a century and a half earlier, could not manage the price of a published volume but could afford the monthly installments. Part issues typically appeared monthly and sold for one shilling, and thus a book in twenty numbers cost considerably less than a triple-decker, which since the appearance of Scott's *Kenilworth* in 1821 had sold for 31s. 6d. A further advantage was that the payment for the novel in numbers was spread out over more than a year and a half.

Serialization had a strong influence on the form of the English novel. Both reviewers and authors were aware that the practice had altered the shape of the genre at some cost; one problem, as a critic noted in the *London Morning Herald* in 1843, was that each installment had to stand as a unit:

> Writers . . . must pay the price of their popularity and submit to be tested by themselves; their noviciate has long passed away, and like practiced actors appearing in a new play, they are expected to be up in their parts, and ready to produce an effect the moment they come on stage. This demand upon them is the more absolute from the manner in which a great proportion of the novels by the most popular writers are now published in separate monthly parts. When, as formerly, the wide range of three volumes lay open to the author to be as dull as he pleased occasionally . . . he had always room enough to redeem himself, when the fit was on him for being effective. But in writing, or rather publishing periodically, the author has no time to be idle; he cannot, as the Irishman did with his bad shilling, smuggle an indifferent (copper) chapter between two good (silver) ones; he must be always lively, pathetic, amusing, or instructive; his pen must never flag—his imagination never tire.[9]

Another reviewer, writing for the *United Service Gazette* in the same year, noted that in the early installments the plot may suffer because the novelist is often busy laying groundwork and developing character:

It is admitted, on all hands, that nothing can be more disadvantageous to the power of a writer than this sort of fragmented mode of publication, and the remark applies, with increased force, to the inaugural part. The last part of the book, containing, as it always does, the *denouement* of the story, is always the most interesting of the whole, and by the same rule the first number must be the dullest.[10]

Frederick Marryat noted the same problem in an essay in the *Metropolitan Magazine* for September 1833:

A narrative may appear in three volumes, and if there is one good chapter out of three, the public are generous and are satisfied; but when every portion is severally presented to be analyzed and criticized for thirty days, the author dare not flag. He must keep up to his mark, or he can never encounter an ordeal so severe.

In a letter to Anna Caroline Wood Steele, Anthony Trollope wrote of the difficulty of serial writing: "Remember that I & a dozen better than I am have to tuck ourselves into contracted limits every month."[11] George Eliot complained of lacking the self-discipline to "drill myself into writing according to set lengths."[12]

Authors and publishers knew that reviews of serial parts could help sales. John Blackwood, fearing that news of Parliament would crowd literary notices out of the newspapers, wrote to George Eliot on his plan for timing the appearance of *Daniel Deronda*: "we think here that the first part should be published before the meeting of Parliament."[13]

The same problems applied to novels published serially in magazines. R. H. Hutton, writing in the *Spectator* in 1863, states his regret "that *Romola* should have been published in fragments" because "George Eliot's drawings all require a certain space, like Raffael's cartoons, and are not of that kind which produce their effect by the reiteration of scenes each complete in itself." The reviewer in the *Athenaeum* makes a similar observation by advising those who had read *Romola* in monthly parts to reread it in the volume edition: "otherwise they may be unable to recognize the many rare merits and beauties which it contains. As a serial story *Romola* was not attractive. . . . "[14] In a letter to William Hardman dated 2 November 1871, George Meredith spoke of his novel *The Adventures of Harry Richmond*, published in the *Cornhill Magazine*: "It struck me that a perusal of the book without enforced pauses might lead you to see that the conception was full and good, and was honestly worked out. I resisted every temptation to produce great and startling effects. . . . " (Meredith's concluding phrase about the use of "startling effects" is a reference to the work of his contemporaries, a topic to be discussed later.) He then mentions his fears that the "enforced pauses" will cause the readers to overlook the subtlety in character development:

Note, as you read, the gradual changes of the growing Harry, in his manner of regarding his father and the world. I have carried it so far as to make him perhaps dull towards adolescence and young manhood, except to one studying the narrative—as in the scenes with Dr. Julius. Such effects are deadly when appearing in a serial issue.[15]

It was perhaps the consciousness that subtlety may be lost on the reader of serial publication and the realization that vivid portraiture is needed to help the audience recall characters from month to month that led Dickens to create characters who are easily visualized or identified with a tag. Hence the reader has a clear image of Pickwick's glasses and gaiters and immediately recognizes Micawber's tag: "I expect something to turn up within the hour."

Composition practices varied. Dickens usually finished each installment four weeks before its appearance but occasionally was as much as a month late.[16] Wilkie Collins seems to have followed the same practice of writing close to the publication deadline, for part 5 of *The Two Destinies* in *Temple Bar* for May 1876 is only half the usual length; an editorial note says, "A sudden attack of illness has prevented the author from proceeding farther with the Number of 'The Two Destinies,' published this month. He has every hope of being able to continue the Story next month in a Number of the customary length."

George Meredith often wrote the entire manuscript before serialization. His contract for *One of Our Conquerors* gave his publishers the right to run it in the *Fortnightly Review* and placed on the author the responsibility to "undertake to reduce the same so that it can be passed through the said Review in not more than seven monthly issues." He faced the same kind of reduction in *Beauchamp's Career*; on 22 May 1874, he wrote to John Morley concerning the need to cut the manuscript for serialization in the *Fortnightly*: "I gladly meet your kind proposal that I should cut it short much as I can, without endangering the arteries. I will get the MS. from George Smith immediately, and do my utmost upon it." After discussing which sections could best be omitted, he concluded, "At any rate they can be reprinted subsequently."[17] The manuscript of *Beauchamp's Career* had been submitted the previous summer and returned to Meredith, who spent most of a year in rewriting it. Even as late as July 1874 he wrote his editor that "The central portion I fear, must be cut to pieces, condensed, re-written."[18]

Anthony Trollope was particularly critical of authors' writing even as serial parts were appearing. In his *Autobiography* he records his reaction to the first offer to publish serially, when he received an invitation from Thackeray to write for the *Cornhill* in 1859:

> And it had already been a principle with me in my art, that no part of a novel should be published till the entire story was completed. I knew, from what I read from month to month, that this hurried publication of incompleted work was frequently, I might perhaps say always, adopted by the leading novelists of the day.

The problem, he said, was that of the farmer driving pigs to market: they would not always go where the farmer intended. So, "When some young lady at the end of a story cannot be made quite perfect in her conduct, that vivid description of angelic purity with which you laid the first lines of her portrait should be toned down." In serialization that early description would have been in print for months, making revision impossible. Thus, he concludes, "I had felt that the rushing mode of publication to which the system of serial stories had given rise, and by which small parts as they were written were sent hot to press, was injurious to the work done."[19] *Framley Parsonage* was Trollope's first serial novel and was the only novel he worked on during its serialization. Having been harried by time pressure, he subsequently always completed each novel before commencing its serial publication. George Meredith in a letter to Julia Duckworth Stephen also referred to this problem of control:

> Diana of the Crossways keeps me still on her sad last way to wedlock. I could have killed her merrily, with my compliments to the public; and that was my intention. But the marrying of her, sets her traversing feminine labyrinths, and you know that the why of it can never be accounted for.[20]

More than half through the serialization of *David Copperfield*, Dickens wrote to his literary confidant, John Forster, that he was uncertain as to the future of David's wife, Dora: "Still undecided about Dora, but MUST decide today."[21] He decided to kill her off.

Critics were sometimes aware, or thought they were, that the novelists were inventing the story as the serial proceeded. At least two authors responded to this criticism. Bulwer-Lytton appended a note to part 11 of *What Will He Do with It?* answering charges that he was unsure of his direction:

> Seeing the length to which this Work has already run, and the space it must yet occupy in the columns of Maga [a nickname for *Blackwood's Magazine*], it is but fair to the Reader to correct any inconsiderable notion that the Author does not know "what he will do with it."

Bulwer's answer is that he had finished the whole novel three months earlier—and a full year before the completion of the serial publication.

Dickens answered a similar criticism raised by Fitzjames Stephen, whose essay "The License of Modern Novelists" in the *Edinburgh Review* accused Dickens of merely borrowing the idea of the collapse of Mrs. Clennam's house from a recent incident of a house falling in the Tottenham Court Road.[22] Responding in *Household Words* Dickens pointed out references early in *Little Dorrit* anticipating the tragedy. That part of the novel had been written and set in type, he declared, before the accident in London occurred.[23]

One danger of writing while serializing was the interruption of the serial. These interruptions resulted from various problems. A quarrel with the proprietor of *Ainsworth's Magazine* led Harrison Ainsworth to cease the publication of *Auriol* in 1845; he republished and completed the novel later the same year in the *New Monthly Magazine*. Poor health sometimes caused an author to miss installments, as when Thackeray's *Pendennis* did not appear for three months in 1848. Dickens' grief over the death of his sister-in-law caused a month's delay in the publication of *Pickwick* in June 1837.

A slightly different interruption occurred in the publication of *Peter Simple* when Frederick Marryat abruptly ended the serial at chapter 42, only two thirds through the novel. In a note appended to the last part Marryat explained that he discontinued the serial so that readers would buy the book. Apparently the public was outraged, because during the publication of his next novel, *Jacob Faithful*, in 1834, he found it necessary to publish this note: "In reply to several letters requesting to know if 'Jacob Faithful' will be finished in the 'Metropolitan,' we state, that such is our intention." Marryat kept his promise.

After Thackeray and Dickens published autobiographical novels in separate serial parts, Ainsworth (having already published eight novels in magazines and newspapers) made his first and only attempt at part publication in 1852 with his autobiographical *Mervyn Clitheroe*. The result was disastrous, and the project was canceled after the fourth number—although resumed five years later—because of the reading public's lack of interest. Part 4 carried a note explaining that a delay would probably occur in the publication, Ainsworth discreetly citing "unforeseen circumstances." It should be noted that the problem was not the mode of publication but the content: Ainsworth's audience had come to expect exciting adventure stories from him, and his autobiography contained no thrilling incidents.

Publication Problems

The tastes of Victorian magazine and newspaper readers sometimes caused difficulties for the editors and owners. In 1863 Norman Macleod, editor of *Good Words*, solicited a novel from Trollope and had actually begun typesetting and advertising *Rachael Ray* when he decided that it was unsuitable for the audience of the magazine. He sent the manuscript back to the author with profuse apologies. Trollope was puzzled at the rejection, writing later that while the novel "is not brilliant . . . it certainly is not very wicked."[24] Hardy encountered a similar problem when he sent part of the manuscript of *Tess of the D'Urbervilles* to Tillotson and Son to be published by the firm's newspaper syndicate. The part, which contained the seduction of Tess and the midnight baptism, was already in proof when Tillotson's asked Hardy to rewrite various sections and delete others. When he refused, the publishing agreement was canceled.

The appearance of novels in magazines gave editors the opportunity to tamper with the text and to make or request modifications before publication. The influence of the editor could be mild, as when Dickens modestly asked Elizabeth Gaskell to change the reading habits of Captain Brown (who, in *Cranford*, was constantly engrossed in the latest installment of *Pickwick*) or when, after reading the manuscript of *Far from the Madding Crowd*, Leslie Stephen apologetically wrote to Hardy:

> I have ventured to leave out a line or two in the last batch of proofs from an excessive prudery of wh. I am ashamed; but one is forced to be absurdly particular. May I suggest that Troy's seduction of the young woman will

require to be treated in a gingerly fashion, when, as I suppose must be the case, he comes to be exposed to his wife? I mean that the thing must be stated but that the words must be careful—excuse this wretched shred of concession to popular stupidity; but I am a slave.[25]

Mowbray Morris, the editor of *Macmillan's Magazine*, was diplomatic when he found it necessary to bowdlerize Hardy's *The Woodlanders*. On 19 September 1886, when the novel was almost halfway through its serialization, Morris wrote to Hardy: "A gentle hint on one small matter— the affair between Miss Damson and the Doctor. . . . I think, if you can contrive not to bring the fair Miss Suke to too open shame, it would be as well. Let the human frailty be construed mild."[26]

Authors' relations with editors, however, were sometimes more difficult. *The Cloister and the Hearth* first appeared in the magazine *Once a Week* under the title *A Good Fight*. The editor irritated Reade by altering the text. The novelist complained, to no avail, until—a serious dispute arising—the editor asked Reade to end the novel as soon as possible. *A Good Fight* is therefore only one-quarter the length of *The Cloister and the Hearth* and has a contrived, unsatisfactory ending. Reade summarized the affair thus:

> I have—"away with melancholy!"—reversed the catastrophe; made Gerard and his sweetheart happy; sent Kate to Heaven, and they and their weekly may go to the other place. Any way the story is finished, and they are rid of me, and I of them—*for ever!*[27]

Editors were always wary of offending the Victorian reading audience. The editor of the *Graphic* found the following passage from part 19 of Wilkie Collins' *The Law and the Lady* unsuitable:

> He caught my hand in his, and devoured it with kisses. His lips burnt me like fire. He twisted himself suddenly in the chair, and wound his arm around my waist. In the terror and indignation of the moment, vainly struggling with him, I cried out for help.

He condensed the paragraph thus:

> He caught my hand in his, and covered it with kisses. In the indignation of the moment I cried out for help.

Collins, noticing the bowdlerization, applied to his solicitor, who in turn communicated with the editor. The following editorial statement resulted:

> The editor of this journal suppressed a portion of the paragraph on the ground that the description as originally given was objectionable. Mr. Wilkie Collins having since informed us, through his legal advisors, that, according to the terms of his agreement with the proprietors of *The Graphic*, his proofs are to be published *verbatim* from his MS., the passage in question is here given in its original form.[28]

After the *Cornhill* rejected one of his stories for being too risqué, Trollope wrote to the editor, Thackeray, saying satirically,

> An impartial Editor must do his duty. Pure morals must be supplied, and the owner of the responsible name must be the Judge of the purity. . . . A

writer for a periodical makes himself subject to this judgment by undertaking such work; and a man who allows himself to be irritated because judgment goes against himself is an ass.

Trollope then proceeds to list scenes and characters from the works of Scott, George Eliot, Dickens, and even Thackeray himself that contain greater "indecencies" than the rejected piece. He concludes, somewhat peevishly, with the statement that he is satisfied "you have used your own judgment impartially & with thoroughly good intention."[29]

Thackeray had established a tradition of purity in the *Cornhill* in the prospectus, "Letter from the Editor to a Friend and Contributor," prefacing the first issue of the magazine in 1860:

> At our social table we shall suppose the ladies and children always present; we shall not set rival politicians by the ears; we shall listen to every guest who has an apt word to say, and I hope to induce clergymen of various denominations to say grace in their turn.

Hardy's *Tess of the D'Urbervilles,* earlier rejected by the Tillotson syndicate, was accepted by the *Graphic,* but before it could be printed the author had to remove Alec's seduction of Tess and substitute a mock marriage. He also had to omit the baptism and death of Tess's baby.[30] When the work appeared as a volume, Hardy was able to present the novel as he originally wrote it, since the standards for books were different from those for serialized fiction in magazines. Editors demanded such bowdlerizations because their magazines were often aimed at family audiences. A writer in *Bow Bells,* a weekly family magazine, sums up the Victorian position and adroitly explains away the bawdiness of the classics:

> One fault which makes itself conspicuous in the works of many writers of the day, is their tendency to touch on topics and open questions which should be avoided. Whatever *is* is a fit subject for the artist, poet, or novelist, is the principle of a certain school, in spite of the teaching of experience that there are hidden realities of life utterly unfit for artistic treatment, and which, however handled, can only debase. A great master—a Shakespeare or a George Eliot—may venture to point a moral from such things; but even in his hands they are painful, and no inferior artist should touch them. But the melancholy fact remains that novels containing this objectionable element find readers; and so long as that is the case moralists may lament and protest in vain. Whether demand creates supply, or supply demand, is a question for the political economists to settle. In either case there is no doubt that increase of appetite is bred by what it feeds on, and a vitiated taste continues to crave for stronger and stronger doses, till the perplexed purveyor of such poisoned food has not a sentiment of modesty left to outrage, nor a law of morality to scoff at. He ransacks heaven and earth for a questionable "situation"; and when he has found it, he rejoices that he can leave his reader tenfold more the child of perdition than before. His sole fear is that he may have been anticipated by some rival dealer in such wares. In truth his novels are mentally what adulterated drink is physically; and in both cases the remedy can only be hoped for in an improved tone of feeling on the subject.[31]

Publishers meddled in other ways. An outrageous example is Kegan's sale of the rights to Meredith's *The Egoist* to the *Glasgow Weekly Herald* without the novelist's permission or knowledge. Meredith was particularly incensed that the newspaper changed the title to *Sir Willoughby Patterne the Egoist*. In a letter Meredith spoke of Kegan's actions, saying "I wrote to him in my incredulous astonishment. He replied to me, excusing himself with cool incompetency. He will have to learn (he is but young at it) that these things may be done once—not more."[32]

Occasionally a novelist would completely rewrite a serialized novel before it appeared in book form. Reade revised *Double Marriage* so extensively that it was impossible for me to indicate the portions of the volume contained in the serial. Other novelists, however, found revision beyond their powers; Dickens said that he had an "insuperable aversion"[33] to revising. Meredith was dissatisfied with *Evan Harrington* in serial, having been barely able to meet the deadlines, and apparently intended to revise it for the volume edition. But he found he could not return to the book, explaining in a letter,

> I wish I could have done more for *Ev[an] Harrington*, for both our sakes: but I should have had to cut him to pieces, put strange herbs to him, and boil him up again—a tortuous and a doubtful process: so I let him go much as *Once a Week* exhibited him.[34]

Serialization often obliged authors to produce parts of uniform length, a requirement that bothered George Eliot. In a letter to her editor, John Blackwood, she discussed the concern they both felt over the fact that book 7 of *Daniel Deronda* was some thirty-five pages shorter than the two previous books. But she concluded that padding for the sake of uniformity was not satisfactory:

> It seemed inadmissible to add anything after the scene with Gwendolyn, and to stick anything in, not necessary to development, between the foregoing chapters, is a form of "matter in the wrong place" particularly repulsive to my authorship's sensibility.[35]

Other writers were not so squeamish. Charles Reade includes a purposeless ghost story in *Put Yourself in His Place* (chapter 11) and pads out three chapters in *A Woman Hater* by having Rhoda Gale tell the story of her life (chapters 12–14). Dickens may have been padding when he inserted tales such as "The Convict's Return" and "The Madman's Manuscript" in *Pickwick*. Advertisements could also fill out serial parts, as G. H. Lewes noted when suggesting that Blackwood's use advertising in the serialized *Middlemarch*: "This would not only bring in some hard cash, it would help the volume look bigger for the 5/—which in British eyes is a consideration not to be neglected."[36]

If the following statement can be taken at face value, the strictures imposed by magazine publication did not bother Hardy in the least, at the beginning of his career. In early 1874 he wrote to Leslie Stephen:

> The truth is that I am willing, and indeed anxious, to give up any points which may be desirable in a story when read as a whole, for the sake of oth-

ers which shall please those who read it in Numbers. Perhaps I may have
higher aims some day, and be a great stickler for the proper artistic balance
of the completed work, but for the present circumstances lead me to wish
merely to be considered a good hand at a serial.[37]

Serialization allowed for anonymous publication, a practice that had
been largely abandoned by the beginning of the Victorian era. In serialization Trollope saw an opportunity for established authors to test the
power of their works disconnected from their names. During the last half
of 1866 he published *Nina Balatka* anonymously in *Blackwood's Magazine*
and found that it would not sell. Undismayed, he published *Linda Tressel*
the next year, also anonymously in *Blackwood's*, only to discover again
that readers seemed to choose their reading material by the author's
name. Trollope published no more novels anonymously.

Dickens' editorial policy, however, required that each piece in *Household Words* appear without an author's name. As a result, an American
publisher put Dickens' name on the title page of *Lizzie Leigh* (actually by
Elizabeth Gaskell) when it was published in the United States.[38]

An important consideration, following the conclusion of the serial, was
the publication of the novel in a three-volume edition. The demand of libraries for three-volume novels perhaps led to the presumption that no
authors were significant unless they wrote long novels. Knowing that
they were required to develop a novel long enough to fill those volumes
must, of course, have had a strong influence on some writers. E. G. Sutcliffe notes that for Charles Reade, who tended toward brief novels, the
effect was disastrous. Sutcliffe adds that Reade's contemporaries—Eliot,
Meredith, Trollope, and Hardy—were convinced that intricate plot struc-
tures were necessary in fiction.[39] But whether that belief developed from
the realization that only a complicated plot could sustain a work for a
thousand pages offers a fertile field for debate.

Those novels not published in the magazines or in monthly numbers
were generally published in three volumes, a practice favored by the circulating libraries because their members would have to purchase two
one-guinea memberships to borrow a complete novel, each membership
allowing the subscriber to borrow only two volumes at a time.[40] When
George Eliot saw that *Middlemarch* would require four rather than the
usual three volumes, G. H. Lewes proposed a unique plan to Blackwood's:

> as you have more than once spoken of the desirability of inventing some
> mode of circumventing the Libraries and making the public *buy* instead of
> borrowing I have devised the following scheme . . . namely to publish it in
> *half-volume parts* either at intervals of one, or as I think better, two months.[41]

Blackwood had earlier said that "This library system I feel to be a false
one. It fosters the production of mediocre novels, but of a really good
book each copy is made to do duty some hundred times over."[42] Blackwood's, therefore, followed Lewes's suggestion, publishing the first five
parts at two-month intervals, the final three at one-month intervals

(again at Lewes's suggestion), in order to have the book completed for the Christmas sales.

Editors realized that certain elements were necessary to sustain interest in serials and that each installment needed these elements. Leslie Stephen, on learning that Thomas Hardy was the author of *Under the Greenwood Tree*, wrote to the novelist describing the kind of story he would like for the *Cornhill Magazine*:

> "Under the Greenwood Tree" is of course not a magazine story. There is too little incident for such purposes; for, though I do not want a murder in every number, it is necessary to catch the attention of readers by some distinct and well arranged plot.[43]

The first part of a serial was particularly important; it was to hook the readers with exciting actions. Dickens wrote to Charles Lever urging him to include more action in the initial installment of *A Day's Ride*, which was to be serialized in *All the Year Round*. Dickens apologized for the suggestion, saying that it arose "solely out of the *manner* of publication."[44]

George Eliot in a letter to John Blackwood also recognized the need for arousing interest in each part. She wrote of *Daniel Deronda*: "But I fear that the present division may make the two first parts—the impression from which is of course supremely important—rather poverty-stricken in point of matter."[45] The division of a novel was sufficiently important to her that she sacrificed considerable money. After agreeing to the publication of *Romola* in the *Cornhill* in sixteen parts for £ 10,000, she decided that the novel could not be divided into so many installments. Instead of subjecting it to such excessive surgery, she agreed to publication in fourteen parts for only £ 7,000.[46]

As editor of *Household Words* Dickens was concerned because Elizabeth Gaskell's *North and South* did not lend itself to serial publication. He wrote to his subeditor: "I am alarmed by the quantity of North and South. It is not objectional, but would become so in the progress of a not compactly written and artfully designed story,"[47] the point being that Gaskell did not grasp the need for significant action in each part. Furthermore, she became adamant about editorial tampering, writing to the subeditor that "she must particularly stipulate not to have her proofs touched 'even by Mr. Dickens.' " Dickens reported that he had nevertheless "gone over the proofs with great pains—had of course taken out the stiflings—hardplungings, lungeings, and other convulsions—and had also taken out her weakenings and damagings of her own effect." He concluded, "Very well . . . she shall have her own way. But after it's published show her this Proof, and ask her to consider whether her story would have been better or worse for it."[48] When, a month and a half into the serialization of *North and South*, the sales of *Household Words* began to decrease, Dickens blamed Gaskell: "I am sorry to hear of the Sale dropping, but I am not surprised. Mrs. Gaskell's story so divided, is wearisome in the last degree."[49]

While serialization hindered Elizabeth Gaskell, it was particularly suitable for the sensation novel of Charles Reade and Wilkie Collins. Collins' definition of the novel and the play as "twin-sisters in the family of fiction," the former being "drama narrated," the latter "drama acted,"[50] led him to believe that the novelist, like the playwright, is privileged to excite strong emotions. A writer in the *Christian Remembrancer* stated that the sensation novel was obligated to contain "something that will induce in the simple idea a sort of thrill."[51] The *Quarterly Review* in 1863 attacked sensation novels for dwelling on scandal, crime (especially murder), bigamy, and adultery.[52] The serial's special suitability for the sensation novel was its periodicity: in addition to exciting the audience with sensational subjects, the novelist could increase the impact by leaving the reader in suspense for a week or a month with thrilling endings of installments.

Endings of Serial Parts

There is perhaps no place in which the process of serialization shows its influence on the novel more than in the endings of serial parts, and the sensation novelists were not the only ones who used serial endings advantageously. George Eliot and George Henry Lewes moved a portion of *Middlemarch* from part 2 to part 1 before publication because it was "a capital bit to end with" and the ending "pitches the interest forward into part II."[53] The serial novelist sometimes tantalized the reader, as Ainsworth did at the conclusion of part 6 of *Hilary St. Ives*: "Mrs. Radcliffe smiled. She thought the housekeeper had done all the mischief she could." The author then adds, "She was very much mistaken." Thackeray uses the same device in part 4 of *Lovel the Widower*: "Elizabeth turned round, gave a little cry, and—but what happened I shall tell in the ensuing chapter." Trollope shunned such suspense in his novels and spoke out against it, facetiously, in *Barchester Towers*, written three years before he began serializing. In chapter 15 as the two repugnant suitors, Obediah Slope and Bertie Stanhope, are maneuvering for advantage with Eleanor Bold, Trollope dispels the mystery: "But let the gentle-hearted reader be under no apprehension. It is not destined that Eleanor shall marry Mr. Slope or Bertie Stanhope." Suspense violates "all proper confidence between the author and his readers," for the reader will expect "delightful horrors" and is led on to the final chapter, which "produces nothing but most commonplace realities." Or worse, Trollope says, the reader fails to exercise self-control and turns to the final chapter to learn the hero's fate or loses a friend who blurts out the vital facts. So he concludes,

> Our doctrine is, that the author and the reader should move along together in full confidence with each other. Let the personages of the drama undergo ever so complete a comedy of errors among themselves, but let the spectator never mistake the Syracusan for the Ephesian; otherwise he is one of the dupes, and the part of the dupe is never dignified.

Occasionally Trollope did employ suspenseful endings. Part 7 of *The Golden Lion of Grampere* concludes thus: "When George was about to undress himself there came a knock at his door, and one of the servant-girls put into his hand a scrap of paper. On it was written, 'I will never marry him, never—never—never; upon my honour!" Part 3 of *Kept in the Dark* finishes with the question, "How was she to tell her husband that she had been engaged to one whom he had described to her as a gambler and a swindler?" Part 23 of *An Eye for an Eye* ends with the chilling statement, "You may call it murder if you please, Father Marty. An eye for an eye, Father Marty! It is justice, and I have done it. 'An Eye for an Eye!' "

George Henry Lewes advised Blackwood's to divide volume 1 of *Daniel Deronda* in such a way that "At each close there is a strong *expectation* excited," which he called "the best of all closes."[54] It is difficult to imagine an ending that could excite greater expectation than the conclusion of part 5 of Charles Reade's *A Good Fight* (later expanded into *The Cloister and the Hearth*): "Their eyes followed hers, and there in the twilight crouched a dark form with eyes like glowworms. It was the leopard!" In the volume edition there is not even a chapter ending at this point. Reade often uses such a captivating device: part 8 ends, "They had never seen a human being killed"; part 9, "a heavy knock fell on the door. And on the hearts within."

Novelists sometimes concluded an installment with a burning question, as Ainsworth did in part 17 of *The South Sea Bubble*: "Could he avoid disgrace? Certain damnatory evidence of his underhand and nefarious proceedings must be removed, or he was lost. He was revolving within his mind how this could be effected, when a tap was heard at the door, and Mr. Knight entered." In case the reader should fail to ask the important questions, Wilkie Collins, as narrator, asks them himself at the end of part 18 of *Blind Love*: "When were they to meet again? And how?"

Frequently the ending delivers a piece of exciting new information to draw the reader back for the next installment to discover how the development came about, as in the conclusion of part 3 of Wilkie Collins' *The New Magdalen*:

> Mercy turned as the sound of the scream rang through the room, and met—resting on her in savage triumph—the living gaze of the woman whose identity she had stolen, whose body she had left laid out for dead. On the instant of that terrible discovery—with her eyes fixed helplessly on the fierce eyes that had found her—she dropped senseless on the floor.

One of the most intriguing bits of information at the end of an installment must be Becky Sharp's reply to Sir Pitt's proposal at the close of part 4 of *Vanity Fair*: " 'Oh, Sir Pitt!' she said. 'Oh, sir—I—I'm *married already.*' "

Charles Reade ended part 2 of *Griffith Gaunt* with information to tantalize the reader, and yet he withheld complete knowledge:

> She tore her way through the last of the snow on to the clear piece, then, white as ashes spurred and lashed her horse over the ridge and dashed in amongst them on the other side. For there they were.
>
> What was the sight that met her eyes?
>
> That belongs to the male branch of my story, and shall be told forthwith but in its proper sequence.

Later, in part 9, the reader was left with this horrifying statement:

> Now, the belief was not yet extinct that the dead body shows some signs of its murderer's approach.
>
> So every eye glared on her and It by turns, as she, with dilated, horror-stricken orbs, looked on that awful Thing.

Reade was particularly concerned with powerful serial endings. The only specific complaint he made about the editor's tampering with the serial of *A Good Fight* in *Once a Week* was that "he confines himself to ending my last number on the feeblest sentence *he* can find out. . . . "[55]

The June 1837 installment of *The Phantom Ship* is only one third the length of the installments preceding and following it. The briefness of the part was necessary, one presumes, so that Marryat could end with this gripping scene: "Philip felt a hand upon his shoulder, and the cold darted through his whole frame. He turned round and met the one eye of Schriften, who screamed in his ear—'PHILIP VANDERDECKEN— That's the *Flying Dutchman!' "*

In spite of Trollope's statement, the Victorian audience enjoyed being dupes, as the great success of Wilkie Collins attests. Collins' formula, "Make 'em cry, make 'em laugh, make 'em wait," made him one of the most successful commercial novelists of the century. A few examples of endings of serial parts, picked almost at random, will display his penchant for suspense:

> Part 8 of *The Law and the Lady*: "The next witnesses called were witnesses concerned with the question that now followed—the obscure and terrible question: Who Poisoned Her?"

> Part 36 of *Man and Wife*: "Geoffrey ran upstairs. Anne followed him. The lad met them at the top of the stairs. He pointed to the open door of Anne's room. She was absolutely certain of having left her lighted candle, when she went down to Geoffrey, at a safe distance from the bedcurtains. The bedcurtains, nevertheless, were in a blaze of flame."

> Part 3 of *Man and Wife*: " 'You can marry me privately to-day,' she answered. 'Listen—and I will tell you how!' "

> Part 27 of *Fallen Leaves*: "He ran into the hall and called to Toff. Was she, by any chance, downstairs? No. Or out in the garden? No. Master and man looked at each other in silence. Sally had gone."

> Part 22 of *The Moonstone*, after Franklin Blake receives the package left behind by the dead Rosanna Spearman: "And, on the unanswerable evidence of the paint-stain, I had discovered Myself as the thief."

> Part 1 of *The Woman in White*: " 'Why are we to stop her, sir? What has she done?' 'Done! She has escaped from my Asylum. Don't forget; a woman in white. Drive on.' "

Sometimes in looking at serial parts one can see clearly that a manuscript was entirely or nearly completed and then sliced into convenient serial portions, with the result that an installment ended at an awkward or illogical point. Part 10 of Charles Reade's *Griffith Gaunt* concludes thus: "The line she took, with one exception, was keen brevity. She cross-examined Thomas Hayes as follows." Various other remnants of serialization remain. Wilkie Collins ended part 23 of *The Woman in White* in the middle of a chapter, opening the next part, a week later, with the phrase "To resume," apparently to draw the reader back into the story after the awkward break in the narrative. This phrase, which served a purpose in the serial, is a useless fixture in the volume edition, a reminder of the original form of publication.

Meredith in revising novels after serialization attempted to smooth the narrative. Part 23 of *Evan Harrington* ends with Juliana's statement " 'I can pardon him,' she said, and sighed. 'How could he love such a face!' " and the omniscient author's remark "I doubt if she really thought so, seeing that she did not pardon him," so that the serial reader had some inkling of what to expect in subsequent installments. After Meredith's revision, this authorial intrusion is missing, apparently because the reader with the complete novel will learn soon enough what Juliana intended to do and, unlike the serial reader, will not have to wait two months for the completion of the work.

In *A Laodicean* Thomas Hardy was able to smooth out the rising ending of a serial part by moving chapter divisions about. Part 6 ends dramatically with terrible news for Mr. Havill:

> "What shall I tell him?" demanded the porter.
> "His wife is dead," said the messenger.

In the volume edition, this revelation falls not at the end of a chapter but in the middle so that there is greater continuity.

Part 11 of Frederick Marryat's *Jacob Faithful* concludes with a statement that seems appropriate for a continuous narrative but not for a serial: "Pass, then, nearly two years, reader, taking the above remarks as an outline, and filling up the picture from the colours of your imagination, with incidents of no peculiar value, and I again resume my narrative." In the volume edition the reader sees the narrative immediately resumed, but in the serial, the reader had to wait a month.

Serialization in magazines was more popular than part issue throughout the century. Of the 192 novels included in the present study, only twenty-five were issued in parts. Part issue met its demise in the 1870s, unable to compete with cheap one-volume reprints and with magazines like the *Cornhill*, which offered installments of two novels and other literature for one shilling. The practice of publishing novels in magazines remained widespread to the end of the nineteenth century and into the twentieth.

Notes

[1] R. M. Wiles in *Serial Publication in England before 1750* (Cambridge: Cambridge Univ. Press, 1957), pp. 80–81, compares *The London Spy* (18 parts, 1698–99) to the *Pickwick Papers*.

²The Act of 10 Anne, c. 19, became effective on 1 Aug. 1712. For a full discussion see Wiles.

³Wiles, p. 33.

⁴See Robert D. Mayo, *The English Novel in the Magazines, 1740–1815* (Evanston: Northwestern Univ. Press, 1962).

⁵Wiles, p. 104.

⁶For a complete list of books published in parts see Wiles's appendix B, "Short-Title Catalogue of Books Published in Facsimile before 1750."

⁷Sam Pickering, Jr., "The First Part-Issue of New Fiction," *English Language Notes*, 12 (1975), 124–27.

⁸Edgar Johnson, *Charles Dickens: His Tragedy and Triumph* (New York: Simon, 1952), I, 149. For a study of the early numbers of the *Pickwick Papers* see J. Don Vann, "The Early Success of Pickwick," *Publishing History*, 2 (1977), 51–55, and Robert L. Patten, "*Pickwick Papers* and the Development of Serial Fiction," *Rice University Studies*, 61 (1975), 51–74.

⁹*London Morning Herald*, 10 Jan. 1843, p. 5.

¹⁰*United Service Gazette*, 21 Jan. 1843, p. 3.

¹¹*The Letters of Anthony Trollope*, ed. Bradford Allen Booth (London: Oxford Univ. Press, 1951), p. 90.

¹²*The George Eliot Letters*, ed. Gordon Haight, VI (New Haven: Yale Univ. Press, 1955), 182.

¹³*George Eliot Letters*, VI, 186.

¹⁴Both reviews are reprinted in *George Eliot: The Critical Heritage*, ed. David Carroll (New York: Barnes and Noble, 1971).

¹⁵*The Letters of George Meredith*, ed. C. L. Cline (Oxford: Oxford Univ. Press, 1970), I, 229.

¹⁶See John Butt, "*David Copperfield*: From Manuscript to Print," *Review of English Studies*, NS 1 (1950), 247–51.

¹⁷Quoted by Maurice Buxton Forman in *A Bibliography of the Writings in Prose and Verse of George Meredith* (Edinburgh: Bibliographical Soc., 1922), p. 52.

¹⁸*Letters of George Meredith*, I, 484.

¹⁹*An Autobiography*, ed. Bradford Allen Booth (Berkeley: Univ. of California Press, 1947), p. 118.

²⁰*Letters of George Meredith*, II, 737.

²¹*The Letters of Charles Dickens*, ed. Walter Dexter (Bloomsbury: Nonesuch, 1938), II, 214.

²²*Edinburgh Review*, 106 (July 1857), 124–56.

²³*Household Words*, 1 Aug. 1857, pp. 97–100.

²⁴*Autobiography*, pp. 156–57. Michael Sadleir gives an account of the incident in *Trollope: A Bibliography* (London: Oxford Univ. Press, 1954), pp. 55–56.

²⁵Richard Little Purdy, *Thomas Hardy: A Bibliographical Study* (London: Oxford Univ. Press, 1954), pp. 338–39.

²⁶Purdy, pp. 55–56.

²⁷Charles L. Reade and Compton Reade, *Charles Reade, Dramatist, Novelist, Journalist: A Memoir Compiled Chiefly from His Literary Remains* (London, 1887), II, 85, 93–95.

²⁸*Graphic*, 30 Jan. 1875, p. 107.

²⁹*Letters of Anthony Trollope*, pp. 77–79.

³⁰Purdy, p. 69.

³¹*Bow Bells*, No. 674 (1877), p. 609.

[32]*Letters of George Meredith,* I, 304.

[33]John Forster, *The Life of Charles Dickens* (London: Chapman and Hall, 1911), I, 437.

[34]*Letters of George Meredith,* I, 171.

[35]*George Eliot Letters,* VI, 240.

[36]*George Eliot Letters,* V, 184.

[37]Florence Emily Hardy, *The Early Life of Thomas Hardy, 1840–1891* (New York: Macmillan, 1928), p. 131.

[38]M. L. Parrish, *Lady Victorian Novelists* (New York: Burt Franklin, 1969), p. 58.

[39]Emerson Grant Sutcliffe, "Plotting in Reade's Novels," *PMLA,* 47 (1932), 834.

[40]For a history of the most famous circulating library see Guinevere L. Griest, *Mudie's Circulating Library and the Victorian Novel* (Bloomington: Indiana Univ. Press, 1970).

[41]*George Eliot Letters,* V, 290.

[42]*George Eliot Letters,* IV, 352.

[43]Purdy, p. 336.

[44]*Letters of Charles Dickens,* III, 165.

[45]*George Eliot Letters,* VI, 181.

[46]George Smith, "Our Birth and Parentage," *Cornhill Magazine,* 83 (Jan. 1901), 10.

[47]*Letters of Charles Dickens,* II, 580.

[48]*Letters of Charles Dickens,* II, 646.

[49]*Letters of Charles Dickens,* II, 598.

[50]Preface to *Basil* (New York: Collier, n.d.), p. 5.

[51]Quoted by W. C. Phillips in *Dickens, Reade, and Collins: Sensation Novelists* (London: Russell and Russell, 1962), p. 26.

[52]*Quarterly Review,* 113 (1863), 481–514.

[53]*George Eliot Letters,* V, 184.

[54]*George Eliot Letters,* VI, 189.

[55]Reade and Reade, II, 94.

William Harrison Ainsworth (1805–82)

Jack Sheppard in *Bentley's Miscellany,* January 1839–February 1840

Part	Date	Chapters in Volume Edition
1	January 1839	"Epoch the First," Chapters 1, 2, 3, 4
2	February	5, 6, 7
3	March	"Epoch the Second," Chapters 1, 2, 3, 4, 5
4	April	6, 7, 8, 9, 10, 11, 12
5	May	13, 14, 15
6	June	16, 17, 18, 19
7	July	"Epoch the Third," Chapters 1, 2, 3, 4
8	August	5, 6, 7, 8
9	September	9, 10, 11, 12
10	October	13
11	November	14, 15, 16
12	December	17, 18, 19, 20, 21, 22, 23
13	January 1840	24, 25, 26, 27
14	February	28, 29, 30, 31, 32

Jack Sheppard was also published in fifteen weekly parts in 1840.

The Tower of London, thirteen parts in twelve monthly installments, January–December 1840

Part	Date	Chapters in Volume Edition
1	January 1840	Book 1, Chapters 1, 2, 3, 4
2	February	5, 6, 7[a]
3	March	7 (cont.), 8, 9, 10, 11
4	April	12, 13, 14, 15, 16, 17; Book 2, Chapters 1, 2, 3
5	May	4, 5, 6, 7
6	June	8, 9, 10, 11
7	July	12, 13, 14, 15, 16
8	August	17, 18, 19, 20
9	September	21, 22, 23, 24, 25
10	October	26, 27, 28, 29

The Tower of London (cont.)

11	November	30, 31, 32, 33
12–13	December	34, 35, 36, 37, 38, 39, 40, 41, 42

*Part 2 ends halfway through chapter 7 with " 'Never!' replied the squire."

The Tower of London was published as a volume in December 1840.

Guy Fawkes in Bentley's Miscellany, January 1840–November 1841

Part	Date	Chapters in Volume Edition
1	January 1840	Book 1, Chapters 1, 2
2	February	3, 4
3	March	5, 6
4	April	7, 8, 9
5	May	10, 11
6	June	12, 13
7	July	14, 15
8	August	16, 17
9	September	18, 19, 20
10	October	Book 2, Chapters 1, 2
11	November	3, 4
12	December	5, 6
13	January 1841	7, 8
14	February	9, 10
15	March	11, 12
16	April	13, 14
17	May	Book 3, Chapters 1, 2
18	June	3, 4
19	July	5, 6
20	August	7, 8
21	September	9, 10, 11
22	October	12, 13
23	November	14, 15, 16, 17

Guy Fawkes was published as a volume in July 1841.

Old Saint Paul's in the *Sunday Times*, 3 January–26 December 1841

Because Ainsworth revised many sections of the novel before its appearance as a volume, it is sometimes impossible to indicate the exact paragraphs that began and ended installments, if only a portion of a chapter was included. The following outline, therefore, gives approximations for parts of chapters.

Part	Date	Chapters in Volume Edition
1	3 January 1841	Book 1, Chapter 1
2	10 January	2
3	17 January	3, 4
4	24 January	5, 6
5	31 January	7, 8
6	7 February	9, 10
7	14 February	Book 2, Chapter 1
8	21 February	2, 3 (first third of chapter)
9	28 February	3 (cont.)
10	7 March	4
11	14 March	5
12	21 March	6
13	28 March	7
14	4 April	8
15	11 April	9
16	18 April	10
17	25 April	11
18	2 May	Book 3, Chapter 1
19	9 May	2 (first half of chapter)
20	16 May	2 (cont.)
21	23 May	3
22	30 May	4 (first half of chapter)
23	6 June	4 (cont.)
24	13 June	5 (first half of chapter)
25	20 June	5 (cont.)
26	27 June	6 (first half of chapter)
27	4 July	6 (cont.)
28	11 July	7
29	18 July	8 (first half of chapter)
30	25 July	8 (cont.)
31	1 August	9
32	8 August	Book 4, Chapter 1 (first half of chapter)

Old Saint Paul's (cont.)

33	15 August	1 (cont.)
34	22 August	2 (first half of chapter)
35	29 August	2 (cont.)
36	5 September	3 (first third of chapter)
37	12 September	3 (middle third of chapter)
38	19 September	3 (cont.)
39	26 September	4
40	3 October	5
41	10 October	6 (first half of chapter)
42	17 October	6 (cont.); Book 5, Chapter 1 (first half of chapter)
43	24 October	1 (cont.)
44	31 October	2
45	7 November	Book 6, Chapter 1
46	14 November	2
47	21 November	3
48	28 November	4
49	5 December	5
50	12 December	6
51	26 December	7, 8, 9, 10

Old Saint Paul's was also published in twelve monthly parts in London in 1841, and it appeared as a volume in December of that year.

The Miser's Daughter in *Ainsworth's Magazine,* January–October 1842

Part	Date	Chapters in Volume Edition
1	January 1842	Book 1, Chapters, 1, 2, 3
2	February	4, 5, 6, 7, 8
3	March	9, 10, 11, 12, 13, 14
4	April	15, 16, 17ª
5	May	17 (cont.), 18, 19, 20; Book 2, Chapters 1, 2
6	June	3, 4

The Miser's Daughter (cont.)

7	July	5, 6, 7, 8, 9, 10, 11
8	August	Book 3, Chapters 1, 2, 3, 4, 5
9	September	6, 7, 8, 9, 10
10	October	11, 12, 13, 14, 15, 16, 17, 18

ᵃPart 4 ends halfway through chapter 17 with " 'I will not!' replied Randulph, firmly. 'It is treasonable, and I refuse it.' "

"As the story neared its serial completion there [in *Ainsworth's Magazine*], at the end of 1842, it was published in three volumes" (S. M. Ellis, *William Harrison Ainsworth and His Friends* [London: John Lane, 1911], II, 50).

Windsor Castle in *Ainsworth's Magazine,* June 1842–June 1843

Part	Date	Chapters in Volume Edition
1	June 1842	Book 1, Chapters 1, 2ᵃ
2	August	3
3	September	4, 5
4	November	8ᵇ
5	December	6, 7, 9, 10
6	January 1843	Book 2, Chapters 1, 2, 3, 4
7	February	5, 6, 7, 8, 9, 10
8	March	Book 4ᶜ, Chapters 1, 2, 3, 4
9	April	5, 6, 7, 8, 9, 10, 11, 12
10	May	Book 3ᶜ, Chapters 1, 2, 3, 4, 5; Book 5, Chapters 1, 2
11	June	3, 4, 5, 6, 7; Book 6, Chapters 1, 2, 3, 4, 5, 6, 7, 8

ᵃThe last three paragraphs of chapter 2 were added after serialization.
ᵇNote the rearrangement of chapters.
ᶜNote the reversal of books 3 and 4.

In 1844 *Windsor Castle* was republished in eleven monthly parts.

St. James's; or, The Court of Queen Anne in *Ainsworth's Magazine*, January–December 1844

Part	Date	Chapters in Volume Edition
1	January 1844	Book 1, Chapters 1, 2, 3, 4[a]
2	February	4 (cont.), 5, 6, 7, 8, 9[b]
3	March	9 (cont.), 10, 11, 12, 13
4	April	14, 15, 16, 17, 18, 19, 20
5	May	Book 2, Chapters 1, 2, 3, 4, 5[c], 7
6	June	6, 8, 9, 10, 11, 12
7	July	Book 3, Chapters 1, 2, 3, 4
8	August	5, 6, 7
9	September	8, 9, 10
10	November[d]	11, 12, 13, 14, 15
11	December	16, 17

[a]Part 1 ends halfway through chapter 4 with "And, with a glance of triumph at the discomfited secretary, she followed the queen into the ball-room."
[b]Part 2 ends slightly less than halfway through chapter 9 with " 'So,' she exclaimed, 'You *are* here, Mr. Harley. . . . Your Majesty does well to give secret audience to this double-dealing trickster.' "
[c]Note the rearrangement of chapters after serialization.
[d]There was no October installment.

St. James's was published as a volume in October 1844.

Auriol; or, The Elixir of Life, published as *Revelations of London* in *Ainsworth's Magazine*, October 1844–May 1845 (partial publication)

Part	Date	Chapters in Volume Edition
1	October 1844	Prologue; Book the First, Chapter 1
2	November	2
3	December	3, 4, 5
4	January 1845	6, 7, 8, 9
5	February	10[a], 11, 12
6	March	"Intermean—1800," Chapters 1, 2

Auriol; or, The Elixir of Life (cont.)

| 7 | April | 3, 4, 5 |
| 8 | May | Book the Second, Chapters 1, 2, 3[b] |

[a]The text of chapter 10 in the volume edition is somewhat reduced from that of the serial.

[b]The serial ends here because Ainsworth, in a dispute with John Mortimer, the owner of the magazine, resigned the editorship and purchased the *New Monthly Magazine*, in which he republished and completed the novel.

Auriol; or, The Elixir of Life in the New Monthly Magazine, July–August 1845

Following his resignation from the editorship of *Ainsworth's Magazine*, Ainsworth purchased the *New Monthly Magazine* in June 1845 and began republishing *Auriol* in July.

Part	Date	Chapters in Volume Edition
1	July 1845	Prologue; Book the First, Chapters 1, 2, 3, 4, 5, 6, 7, 8, 9, 10[a], 11, 12; "Intermean—1800," Chapters 1, 2, 3, 4, 5; Book the Second, Chapters 1, 2, 3
2	August	Book the Second, Chapters 4, 5[b]

[a]Chapter 10 of book 1, which had appeared in briefer form in *Ainsworth's Magazine*, was expanded to its final form for the *New Monthly Magazine* serialization.

[b]Chapter 6 of book 2 was not included in the serial.

The Lancaster Witches in the Sunday Times, 2 January 1848–7 January 1849

This novel, like *Old Saint Paul's*, was revised before the volume publication, making it difficult to indicate the exact content of each installment.

Part	Date	Chapters in Volume Edition
1	2 January 1848	Introduction, Chapters 1, 2
2	9 January	3, 4

The Lancaster Witches (cont.)

3	16 January	5, 6, 7 (first third of chapter)
4	23 January	7 (cont.), 8, 9, 10, 11
5	30 January	Book 1, Chapters 1, 2
6	6 February	3
7	13 February	4
8	20 February	5 (first half of chapter)
9	27 February	5 (cont.)
10	5 March	6
11	12 March	7 (first half of chapter)
12	19 March	7 (cont.)
13	26 March	8
14	2 April	9 (first third of chapter)
15	9 April	9 (middle third of chapter)
16	16 April	9 (cont.)
17	23 April	10 (first half of chapter)
18	7 May	10 (cont.)
19	14 May	Book 2, Chapter 1
20	21 May	2, 3
21	28 May	4
22	4 June	5
23	11 June	6
24	18 June	7 (first half of chapter)
25	25 June	7 (cont.)
26	2 July	8
27	9 July	9 (first half of chapter)
28	16 July	9 (cont.)
29	23 July	10
30	30 July	11 (first third of chapter)
31	6 August	11 (cont.)
32	13 August	12 (first three quarters of chapter)
33	20 August	12 (cont.), 15
34	27 August	14
35	3 September	13 (first half of chapter)
36	10 September	13 (cont.)
37	17 September	16
38	24 September	17
39	1 October	Book 3, Chapter 1 (first half of chapter)
40	8 October	1 (cont.)

The Lancaster Witches (cont.)

41	15 October	2
42	22 October	3
43	29 October	4
44	5 November	5
45	12 November	6 (first half of chapter)
46	19 November	6 (cont.)
47	26 November	7
48	3 December	8
49	17 December	9
50	24 December	10
51	31 December	11, 12
52	7 January 1849	13, 14, 15

"About the time *The Lancaster Witches* completed serial appearance in *The Sunday Times*, Ainsworth had a few copies of the story printed off from the newspaper type, and these, bound in a folio volume with pages of two columns, he presented to his friends; this was the first edition. . . . The second (and first public) edition, in three volumes, was published early in 1849 by Colburn" (Ellis, II, 163).

Mervyn Clitheroe, twelve parts in eleven monthly installments, December 1851–March 1852, December 1857–June 1858

Part	Date	Chapters in Volume Edition
1	December 1851	Book the First, Chapters 1, 2, 3, 4
2	January 1852	5, 6, 7, 8
3	February	9, 10, 11
4	March	12, 13, 14, 15[a]
5	December 1857	Book the Second, Chapters 1, 2, 3, 4
6	January 1858	5, 6, 7, 8
7	February	9, 10, 11, 12
8	March	13, 14, 15; Book the Third, Chapter 1
9	April	2, 3, 4
10	May	5, 6, 7, 8, 9, 10, 11, 12
11–12	June	13, 14, 15, 16, 17, 18, 19, 20

[a]At the end of part 4 is this notice: "The first part of the ADVENTURES OF MERVYN CLITHEROE—'part of a whole, yet in itself complete'—is now concluded. Some delay will probably occur in the continuation of the Story. The Author regrets it, but the delay is unavoidable on his part. Unforeseen circumstances are likely to

compel him to suspend, for awhile, his pleasant task;—pleasant, because many of the
incidents and characters have been supplied to him by his own personal
recollections, while the scenes in which the events are placed have been familiar to
him since childhood. Ere long he hopes to meet his friends again; bidding them,
meanwhile, a kindly farewell!"

The first four parts were published by Chapman and Hall, the others by George
Routledge and Company. Routledge reissued the first four parts in wrappers to
match the later parts.

The Star Chamber in the *Home Companion,* 16 April–31 December 1853

Part	Date	Chapters in Volume Edition
1	16 April 1853	1, 2
2	23 April	3, 4
3	30 April	5, 6
4	7 May	7, 8
5	14 May	9
6	21 May	10, 11
7	28 May	12
8	4 June	13
9	11 June	14
10	18 June	15, 16
11	25 June	17, 18
12	2 July	19
13	9 July	20
14	16 July	21
15	23 July	22
16	30 July	23
17	6 August	24, 25
18	13 August	26
19	20 August	27, 28
20	27 August	29
21	3 September	30, 31
22	10 September	32, 33
23	17 September	34
24	24 September	35, 36

The Star Chamber (cont.)

25	1 October	37, 38
26	8 October	39, 40
27	15 October	41, 42
28	22 October	43, 44
29	29 October	45, 46
30	5 November	47, 48
31	12 November	49, 50
32	19 November	51, 52
33	26 November	53
34	3 December	54, 55
35	10 December	56, 57, 58
36	17 December	59
37	31 December[a]	60, 61, 62

[a]There was no installment in the 24 December issue.

"The first edition, in two volumes, was published early in 1854" (Ellis, II, 190).

The Flitch of Bacon in the *New Monthly Magazine*, January 1853– May 1854

Part	Date	Chapters in Volume Edition
1	January 1853	Part the First, Chapters 1, 2, 3, 4, 5, 6
2	February	7, 8, 9, 10
3	March	Part the Second, Chapters 6[a], 2, 1, 3
4	April	4, 5; Part the Third, Chapters 1, 2
5	May	Part the Second, Chapters 7, 8
6	April 1854[b]	Part the Fourth, Chapters 1, 2, 3, 4
7	May	5; Part the Fifth, Chapters 1, 2, 3, 4, 5, 6

[a]Note the rearrangement of chapters.
[b]I have been unable to discover the reason for the pause in publication.

The Flitch of Bacon was published as a volume in May 1854.

The Spendthrift in *Bentley's Miscellany*, January 1855–January 1857

Part	Date	Chapters in Volume Edition
1	January 1855	1, 2, 3, 4
2	February	5
3	March	6, 7
4	April	8, 9, 10, 11
5	May	12, 13, 14
6	November*	15
7	December	16, 17, 18, 19
8	January 1856	20, 21, 22
9	February	23
10	March	24, 25
11	April	26
12	May	27, 28, 29
13	July*	30, 31
14	August	32, 33, 34, 35
15	September	36, 37, 38
16	October	39, 40, 41
17	November	42, 43, 44
18	December	45, 46, 47, 48, 49, 50
19	January 1857	51, 52

*Whether these gaps in serialization were caused by illness or the press of business is not known.

The Spendthrift was published as a volume in December 1856.

Ovingdean Grange: A Tale of the South Downs in *Bentley's Miscellany*, November 1859–July 1860

Part	Date	Chapters in Volume Edition
1	November 1859	Book the First, Chapters 1, 2, 3
2	December	Book the Second, Chapters 1, 2, 3

Ovingdean Grange (cont.)

3	January 1860	Book the Third, Chapters 1, 2, 3, 4
4	February	Book the Fourth, Chapters 1, 2, 3, 4, 5
5	March	Book the Fifth, Chapters 1, 2, 3, 4, 5
6	April	Book the Sixth, Chapters 1, 2, 3, 4, 5, 6
7	May	Book the Seventh, Chapters 1, 2, 3, 4, 5, 6, 7
8	June	Book the Eighth, Chapters 1, 2, 3, 4, 5, 6, 7, 8
9	July	9, 10, 11; Book the Ninth, Chapters 1, 2, 3, 4; L'Envoi

"On its completion there [in *Bentley's Miscellany*] it was published by Routledge" (Ellis, II, 231).

The Constable of the Tower in *Bentley's Miscellany*, January–September 1861

Part	Date	Chapters in Volume Edition
1	January 1861	Prologue, Chapters 1, 2, 3, 4, 5, 6
2	February[a]	7, 8; Book the First, Chapters 1, 2, 3, 4
3	March[b]	5, 6, 7, 8, 9, 10, 11
4	April	12, 13, 14, 15, 16, 17, 18, 19
5	May	Book the Second, Chapters 1, 2, 3, 4, 5, 6, 7, 8, 9
6	June	10, 11, 12, 13, 14[c], 16, 15[d], 17
7	July	Book the Third, Chapters 1, 2, 3, 4, 5, 6, 7, 8, 9
8	August	10; Book the Fourth, Chapters 1, 2
9	September	3, 4, 5, 6

[a]The February issue of *Bentley's Miscellany* reprinted reviews of the first installment of *The Constable of the Tower* from the *Examiner* and the *London Review*.
[b]The March issue reprinted a review from the *London Review*.
[c]The first few paragraphs of chapter 14 were revised after serialization.
[d]Note that chapters 15 and 16 were published in reverse order in the serial.

The Lord Mayor of London; or, City Life in the Last Century in Bentley's Miscellany, January–November 1862

Part	Date	Chapters in Volume Edition
1	January 1862	Book the First, Chapters 1, 2, 3
2	February	4, 5, 6, 7, 8
3	March	9, 10, 11, 12, 13, 14
4	April	15, 16, 17, 18, 19
5	May	Book the Second, Chapters 1, 2, 3, 4, 5, 6, 7
6	June	Book the Third, Chapters 1, 2, 3, 4, 5, 6, 7, 8
7	July	9, 10, 11, 12, 13, 14, 15, 16, 17, 18, 19
8	August	Book the Fourth, Chapters 1, 2, 3, 4, 5, 6, 7
9	September	8, 9, 10, 11, 12
10	October	13, 14; Book the Fifth, Chapters 1, 2
11	November	3, 4; Epilogue

Cardinal Pole; or, The Days of Philip and Mary in Bentley's Miscellany, December 1862–November 1863

Part	Date	Chapters in Volume Edition
1	December 1862	Book the First, Chapters 1, 2, 3
2	January 1863	4, 5, 6, 7, 8, 9
3	February	10, 11, 12, 13, 14, 15, 16
4	March	Book the Second, Chapters 1, 2, 3, 4, 5
5	April	6, 7, 8; Book the Third, Chapters 1, 2[a]
6	May	Book the Second, Chapters 9, 10, 11; Book the Third, Chapters 3, 4
7	June	5, 6, 7, 8, 9, 10, 11, 12
8	July	13; Book the Fourth, Chapters 1, 2, 3, 4, 5
9	August	Book the Fifth, Chapters 1, 2, 3, 4, 5, 6, 7, 8
10	September	Book the Sixth, Chapters 1, 2, 3, 4, 5, 6
11	October	Book the Seventh, Chapters 1, 2, 3, 4, 5, 6, 7
12	November	Book the Eighth, Chapters 1, 2, 3

[a]Note that chapters 1 and 2 of book 3 were published out of sequence in the serial.

Cardinal Pole was published as a volume in July 1863.

John Law in *Bentley's Miscellany,* November 1863–September 1864

Part	Date	Chapters in Volume Edition
1	November 1863	Prologue, Chapters 1, 2, 3, 4, 5
2	December	6, 7, 8, 9, 10, 11, 12
3	January 1864	Book 1, Chapters 1, 2, 3, 4, 5
4	February	Book 2, Chapters 1, 2, 3, 4, 5, 6, 7, 8, 9
5	March	Book 3, Chapters 1, 2, 3; Book 4, Chapters 1, 2
6	April	3, 4, 5, 6, 7
7	May	8, 9, 10, 11; Book 5, Chapters 1, 2, 3, 4, 5, 6
8	June	7, 8, 9, 10, 11, 12; Book 6, Chapters 1, 2
9	July	3, 4, 5, 6; Book 7, Chapters 1, 2, 3, 4, 5, 6, 7
10	August	8, 9, 10, 11, 12; Book 8, Chapters 1, 2, 3, 4, 5, 6
11	September	7, 8, 9, 10, 11; L'Envoi

The Spanish Match, published as *The House of Seven Chimneys* in *Bentley's Miscellany,* November 1864–October 1865

Part	Date	Chapters in Volume Edition
1	November 1864	Book 1, Chapters 1, 2, 3
2	December	4, 5, 6, 7, 8, 9
3	January 1865	10, 11, 12, 13
4	February	14, 15, 16, 17, 18, 19
5	March	20, 21, 22, 23, 24
6	April	25; Book 2, Chapters 1, 2, 3; Book 3, Chapter 1
7	May	2, 3, 4, 5, 6, 7, 8, 9
8	June	Book 4, Chapters 1, 2, 3, 4, 5, 6, 7, 8, 9
9	July	10, 11, 12; Book 5, Chapters 1, 2, 3, 4
10	August	5, 6, 7, 8, 9; Book 6, Chapters 1, 2, 3, 4
11	October	Book 7, Chapters 1, 2, 3, 4, 5, 6

The Constable de Bourbon in *Bentley's Miscellany,* November 1865–August 1866

Part	Date	Chapters in Volume Edition
1	November 1865	Book 1, Chapters 1, 2, 3, 4, 5; Book 2, Chapters 1, 2, 3, 4
2	December	5, 6, 7, 8, 9, 10, 11, 12, 13
3	January 1866	14, 15, 16, 17, 18, 19
4	February	Book 3, Chapters 1, 2, 3, 4, 5, 6, 7, 8, 9
5	March	Book 4, Chapters 1, 2, 3, 4
6	April	5, 6, 7, 8, 9, 10, 11, 12, 13, 14
7	May	15; Book 5, Chapters 1, 2, 3, 4, 5
8	June	6, 7, 8, 9, 10, 11, 12
9	July	Book 6, Chapters 1, 2; Book 7, Chapters 1, 2, 3, 4
10	August	5, 6, 7, 8, 9, 10

Old Court in *Bentley's Miscellany,* October 1866–May 1867

Part	Date	Chapters in Volume Edition
1	October 1866	Prologue, Chapters 1, 2, 3, 4, 5, 6, 7
2	November	8, 9; Book 1, Chapters 1, 2, 3, 4, 5
3	December	6, 7; Book 2, Chapters 1, 2, 3, 4, 5, 6
4	January 1867	Book 3, Chapters 1, 2, 3, 4, 5, 6, 7, 8, 9, 10, 11, 12, 13
5	February	Book 4, Chapters 1, 2, 3, 4, 5, 6, 7, 8
6	March	9, 10, 11, 12, 13, 14, 15
7	April	Book 5, Chapters 1, 2, 3, 4, 5, 6, 7, 8, 9
8	May	Book 6, Chapters 1, 2, 3, 4, 5, 6, 7, 8, 9

Myddleton Pomfret in *Bentley's Miscellany,* July 1867–March 1868

Part	Date	Chapters in Volume Edition
1	July 1867	Prologue, Chapters 1, 2; Book 1, Chapters 1, 2, 3, 4
2	August	Book 2, Chapters 1, 2, 3, 4, 5, 6

Myddleton Pomfret (cont.)

3	September	Book 3, Chapters 1, 2, 3, 4, 5, 6, 7, 8, 9
4	October	10, 11; Book 4, Chapters 1, 2, 3
5	November	4, 5, 6, 7; Book 5, Chapters 1, 2, 3
6	December	4, 5, 6, 7, 8, 9, 10, 11, 12, 13; Book 6, Chapters 1, 2, 3
7	January 1868	4, 5, 6, 7, 8, 9, 10, 11
8	February	12, 13, 14, 15, 16, 17, 18, 19
9	March	Book 7, Chapters 1, 2

The South Sea Bubble in *Bow Bells*, 1 July–11 November 1868

Part	Date	Chapters in Volume Edition
1	1 July 1868	Prologue, Chapters 1, 2, 3, 4
2	8 July	5, 6, 7
3	15 July	8, 9
4	22 July	10, 11; Book 1, Chapter 1
5	29 July	2, 3, 4
6	5 August	5, 6
7	12 August	7, 8
8	19 August	9, 10, 11
9	26 August	12, 13, 14, 15, 16
10	2 September	17, 18, 19, 20
11	9 September	21, 22, 23, 24
12	16 September	25, 26, 27
13	23 September	Book 2, Chapters 1, 2, 3
14	30 September	4, 5
15	7 October	6, 7, 8
16	14 October	9, 10, 11
17	21 October	12, 13; Book 3, Chapter 1
18	28 October	2, 3, 4
19	4 November	5, 6, 7, 8
20	11 November	9, 10, 11, 12, L'Envoi

The South Sea Bubble was published as a volume in June 1871.

Hilary St. Ives in the New Monthly Magazine, February–December 1869

Part	Date	Chapters in Volume Edition
1	February 1869	Book 1, Chapters 1, 2, 3, 4
2	March	5, 6, 7, 8, 9, 10, 11, 12
3	April	13, 14, 15, 16, 17, 18, 19
4	May	Book 2, Chapters 1, 2, 3, 4, 5, 6, 7
5	June	8, 9, 10, 11, 12, 13, 14
6	July	15, 16, 17, 18
7	August	19, 20, 21, 22, 23, 24, 25; Book 3, Chapter 1
8	September	2, 3, 4, 5, 6
9	October	7, 8, 9
10	November	10, 11, 12, 13, 14, 15, 16
11	December	17, 18, 19

Talbot Harland in Bow Bells, 4 May–27 July 1870

Part	Date	Chapters in Volume Edition
1	4 May 1870	Book 1, Chapters 1, 2, 3, 4, 5, 6
2	11 May	7, 8, 9, 10, 11, 12, 13
3	18 May	14, 15, 16, 17, 18
4	25 May	19, 20, 21, 22, 23
5	1 June	24, 25; Book 2, Chapters 1, 2, 3
6	8 June	4, 5, 6, 7
7	15 June	8, 9, 10, 11
8	22 June	Book 3, Chapters 1, 2, 3, 4, 5, 6, 7
9	29 June	8, 9, 10, 11, 12, 13
10	6 July	14, 15, 16, 17
11	13 July	Book 4, Chapters 1, 2, 3, 4, 5
12	20 July	Book 5, Chapters 1, 2, 3, 4, 5
13	27 July	6, 7, 8

Tower Hill in *Bow Bells*, 1 February–26 April 1871

Part	Date	Chapters in Volume Edition
1	1 February 1871	Book 1, Chapters 1, 2, 3
2	8 February	4, 5, 6
3	15 February	7, 8, 9, 10, 11
4	22 February	12, 13, 14, 15
5	1 March	Book 2, Chapters 1, 2, 3, 4, 5
6	8 March	6, 7, 8, 9, 10
7	15 March	11; Book 3, Chapters 1, 2
8	22 March	3, 4, 5, 6, 7
9	29 March	8, 9, 10, 11, 12, 13, 14, 15, 16
10	5 April	17, 18, 19, 20, 21, 22
11	12 April	23, 24, 25, 26, 27, 28
12	19 April	29, 30, 31
13	26 April	32

Boscobel in the *New Monthly Magazine*, January–December 1872

Part	Date	Chapters in Volume Edition
1	January 1872	Book 1, Chapters 1, 2, 3, 4, 5, 6
2	February	7, 8, 9, 10, 11, 12, 13, 14
3	March	15, 16, 17, 18, 19, 20, 21
4	April	22, 23, 24, 25, 26, 27, 28, 29, 30, 31, 32
5	May	Book 2, Chapters 1, 2, 3, 4, 5, 6, 7, 8
6	June	Book 3, Chapters 1, 2, 3, 4, 5, 6, 7, 8, 9, 10, 11
7	July	Book 4, Chapters 1, 2, 3, 4, 5, 6, 7, 8
8	August	Book 5, Chapters 1, 2, 3, 4, 5, 6, 7, 8, 9, 10
9	September	Book 6, Chapters 1, 2, 3, 4, 5, 6, 7, 8, 9
10	October	Book 7, Chapters 1, 2, 3, 4, 5, 6, 7, 8, 9, 10
11	November	11, 12, 13, 14, 15, 16, 17, 18
12	December	19, 20, 21, 22, 23, 24, 25

Boscobel was published as a volume in October 1872.

Merry England in *Bow Bells*, 7 January–22 April 1874

Part	Date	Chapters in Volume Edition
1	7 January 1874	Book 1, Chapters 1, 2, 3, 4
2	14 January	5, 6, 7, 8, 9, 10
3	21 January	11, 12, 13, 14, 15, 16, 17
4	28 January	18, 19, 20, 21, 22, 23, 24, 25
5	4 February	26, 27, 28, 29, 30, 31, 32
6	11 February	33, 34, 35, 36, 37, 38
7	18 February	Book 2, Chapters 1, 2, 3, 4, 5
8	25 February	6, 7, 8, 9, 10
9	4 March	11, 12, 13, 14, 15
10	11 March	16, 17, 18, 19, 20
11	18 March	Book 3, Chapters 1, 2, 3, 4, 5
12	25 March	6, 7, 8, 9, 10, 11
13	1 April	12, 13; Book 4, Chapters 1, 2
14	8 April	3, 4, 5, 6
15	15 April	7; Book 5, Chapters 1, 2, 3, 4, 5
16	22 April	6, 7, 8, 9, 10

The Goldsmith's Wife in *Bow Bells*, 16 September 1874–6 January 1875

Part	Date	Chapters in Volume Edition
1	16 September 1874	Book 1, Chapters 1, 2, 3, 4, 5
2	23 September	6, 7, 8, 9, 10
3	30 September	11, 12, 13, 14, 15
4	7 October	16; Book 2, Chapters 1, 2
5	14 October	3, 4, 5, 6, 7
6	21 October	8, 9, 10
7	28 October	11, 12, 13, 14, 15
8	4 November	16, 17, 18, 19, 20
9	11 November	Book 3, Chapters 1, 2, 3, 4

The Goldsmith's Wife (cont.)

10	18 November	5, 6, 7, 8, 9
11	25 November	10; Book 4, Chapters 1, 2, 3
12	2 December	4, 5, 6, 7, 8, 9
13	9 December	10, 11
14	16 December	Book 5, Chapters 1, 2, 3, 4
15	23 December	5; Book 6, Chapters 1, 2, 3
16	30 December	4, 5; Book 7, Chapters 1, 2, 3
17	6 January 1875	4, 5, 6

Chetwynd Calverley in *Bow Bells*, 12 April–26 July 1876

Part	Date	Chapters in Volume Edition
1	12 April 1876	Introduction, Chapters 1, 2, 3, 4, 5, 6, 7
2	19 April	8; Book 1, Chapters 1, 2, 3, 4, 5, 6
3	26 April	7, 8, 9, 10, 11, 12, 13
4	3 May	14, 15; Book 2, Chapters 1, 2, 3
5	10 May	4; Book 3, Chapters 1, 2, 3, 4
6	17 May	5, 6, 7, 8, 9
7	24 May	10; Book 4, Chapters 1, 2, 3, 4
8	31 May	5, 6, 7, 8, 9, 10
9	7 June	Book 5, Chapters 1, 2, 3, 4, 5
10	14 June	6, 7, 8, 9, 10, 11
11	21 June	12, 13, 14, 15
12	28 June	16; Book 6, Chapters 1, 2, 3, 4, 5
13	5 July	6, 7, 8, 9, 10, 11, 12
14	12 July	13, 14, 15, 16, 17
15	19 July	18, 19, 20, 21, 22, 23
16	26 July	24, 25, 26, 27, 28, 29

Chetwynd Calverley was published as a volume in June 1876.

The Fall of Somerset in *Bow Bells,* 25 April–15 August 1877

Part	Date	Chapters in Volume Edition
1	25 April 1877	Book 1, Chapters 1, 2, 3
2	2 May	4, 5, 6, 7, 8
3	9 May	9, 10, 11, 12
4	16 May	13, 14, 15, 16, 17
5	23 May	18, 19, 20, 21, 22
6	30 May	23, 24, 25, 26, 27, 28
7	6 June	Book 2, Chapters 1, 2, 3, 4ᵃ
8	13 June	4 (cont.), 5, 6, 7, 8
9	20 June	9, 10, 11, 12, 13
10	27 June	14, 15, 16, 17
11	4 July	18, 19, 20, 21, 22
12	11 July	23; Book 3, Chapters 1, 2, 3, 4
13	18 July	5, 6, 7, 8, 9
14	25 July	10, 11, 12, 13, 14, 15
15	1 August	16, 17, 18, 19, 20, 21
16	8 August	22, 23, 24, 25
17	15 August	26, 27, 28, 29, 30

ᵃPart 7 ends two thirds of the way through chapter 4 with " 'After all, I believe we shall have a satisfactory explanation of the mystery,' she said. 'But I will await the duke's return before taking any further steps.' "

Beatrice Tyldesley in *Bow Bells,* 30 January–15 May 1878

Part	Date	Chapters in Volume Edition
1	30 January 1878	Introduction, Chapters 1, 2, 3, 4
2	6 February	5, 6, 7, 8, 9, 10
3	13 February	11, 12, 13; Book 1, Chapters 1, 2
4	20 February	3, 4, 5, 6, 7, 8, 9
5	27 February	10, 11, 12, 13
6	6 March	14; Book 2, Chapters 1, 2, 3, 4
7	13 March	5, 6, 7, 8, 9
8	20 March	10, 11, 12; Book 3, Chapter 1
9	27 March	2, 3, 4, 5

Beatrice Tyldesley (cont.)

10	3 April	6, 7, 8, 9
11	10 April	10, 11, 12, 13; Book 4, Chapter 1
12	17 April	2, 3, 4, 5
13	24 April	6, 7, 8
14	1 May	9, 10, 11, 12
15	8 May	13, 14, 15, 16
16	15 May	17, 18, 19, 20, 21, 22

Beatrice Tyldesley was published as a volume in April 1878.

Stanley Brereton in the *Bolton Weekly Journal*, 26 February–13 August 1881

Part	Date	Chapters in Volume Edition
1	26 February 1881	Prologue, 1, 2, 3
2	5 March	4, 5, 6
3	12 March	7, 8, 9
4	19 March	10, 11, 12
5	26 March	13, 14, 15, 16
6	2 April	17, 18, 19
7	9 April	20, 21, 22
8	16 April	23, 24, 25
9	23 April	26, 27, 28, 29
10	30 April	30, 31, 32
11	7 May	33, 34, 35
12	14 May	36, 37, 38, 39, 40
13	21 May	41, 42, 43, 44
14	28 May	45, 46, 47, 48
15	4 June	49, 50, 51
16	11 June	52, 53, 54, 55, 56
17	18 June	57, 58, 59, 60
18	25 June	61, 62, 63
19	2 July	64, 65, 66
20	9 July	67, 68, 69, 70, 71

Stanley Brereton (cont.)

21	16 July	72, 73, 74, 75
22	23 July	76, 77
23	30 July	78, 79, 80
24	6 August	81, 82, 83, 84
25	13 August	85, 86, 87, 88, 89, 90, 91, 92

William Wilkie Collins (1824–89)

A Rogue's Life in *Household Words,* 1 March–29 March 1856

Part	Date	Chapters in Volume Edition
1	1 March 1856	1, 2, 3
2	8 March	4, 5, 6
3	15 March	7, 8, 9
4	22 March	10, 11, 12
5	29 March	13, 14, 15, 16, Postscript

The Dead Secret in *Household Words,* 3 January–13 June 1857

Part	Date	Chapters in Volume Edition
1	3 January 1857	Book 1, Chapter 1
2	10 January	2, 3
3	17 January	Book 2, Chapter 1
4	24 January	2
5	31 January	3
6	7 February	Book 3, Chapter 1
7	14 February	2, 3
8	21 February	4
9	28 February	5, 6
10	7 March	Book 4, Chapter 1
11	14 March	2
12	21 March	3
13	28 March	4
14	11 April	5
15	18 April	Book 5, Chapters 1, 2
16	25 April	3, 4
17	2 May	5[a]
18	9 May	5 (cont.), 6
19	16 May	Book 6, Chapter 1
20	23 May	2
21	30 May	3

The Dead Secret (cont.)

| 22 | 6 June | 4 |
| 23 | 13 June | 5, 6 |

ªPart 17 ends thirty paragraphs short of the end of chapter 5, the last paragraph beginning "It was getting on toward noon" and ending "she took up the paper from the table, and opened it."

The Dead Secret was published as a volume in June 1857.

The Woman in White in *All the Year Round,* 26 November 1859–25 August 1860

Part	Date	Chapters in Volume Edition
1	26 November 1859	"The Story Begun by Walter Hartright," Chapters 1, 2, 3, 4
2	3 December	5, 6, 7
3	10 December	8
4	17 December	9, 10
5	24 December	11, 12
6	31 December	13
7	7 January 1860	14, 15
8	14 January	"The Story Continued by Vincent Gilmore," Chapters 1, 2
9	21 January	3, 4
10	28 January	"The Story Continued by Marian Holcombe," Chapter 1
11	4 February	2
12	11 February	"The Second Epoch. The Story Continued by Marian Holcombe," Chapter 1
13	18 February	2
14	25 February	3
15	3 March	4
16	10 March	5
17	17 March	6ª
18	24 March	6 (cont.)
19	31 March	7

The Woman in White (cont.)

20	7 April	8, 9[b]
21	14 April	9 (cont.)
22	21 April	10; "The Story Continued by Frederick Fairlie"[c]
23	28 April	"Fairlie" (cont.); "The Story Continued by Eliza Michelson," Chapter 1[d]
24	5 May	1 (cont.)
25	12 May	2[e]
26	19 May	2 (cont.) "The Story Continued in Several Narratives," "Hester Pinhorn," "The Doctor," "The Tombstone," "The Narrative of Walter Hartright"
27	26 May	"The Third Epoch. The Story Continued by Walter Hartright," Chapters 1, 2[f]
28	2 June	2 (cont.), 3
29	9 June	4
30	16 June	5, 6
31	23 June	7
32	30 June	8
33	7 July	9
34	14 July	10
35	21 July	11; "The Story Continued by Mrs. Catherick"[g]
36	28 July	"Mrs. Catherick" (cont.); "The Story Continued by Walter Hartright," Chapter 1
37	4 August	2
38	11 August	3, 4, 5
39	18 August	6, 7
40	25 August	"The Story Continued by Isidor, Ottavio, Baldassare Fosco"; "The Story Concluded by Walter Hartright," Chapters 1, 2, 3

[a]Part 17 ends almost halfway through the chapter with the following conversation: " 'Who, for Heaven's sake?' 'Anne Catherick.' "

[b]Only the first five paragraphs of chapter 9 are included in part 20.

[c]Part 22 ends halfway through Fairlie's section with "Gracious Heaven! my tiresome sister's foreign husband. Count Fosco."

[d]Part 23 ends one fourth of the way through the first chapter with the paragraph beginning "I proceeded upstairs" and ending "The only question I asked myself was—Had he found her?"

[e]Part 25 ends two thirds of the way through chapter 2 with "Miss Halcombe, ma'am, has not left Blackwater Park, either."

[f]Part 27 ends three fifths of the way through chapter 2 with the paragraph beginning "During the latter part of their journey they were alone in the carriage"

and ending "this explanatory narrative closes with the events of the next day at Limmeridge House."

ᵍPart 35 ends halfway through the "Mrs. Catherick" section with the paragraph beginning "So I accepted the conditions he offered me. . . . " The part ends in the middle of the paragraph with "I will turn to a fresh page and give you the answer immediately."

The Woman in White was also serialized in *Harper's* from 26 November 1859 to 8 September 1860. The outline above reflects revisions Collins made in 1860 for the volume edition; all modern editions follow the revised text except for the Oxford edition (ed. H. P. Sucksmith) and the Riverside edition (ed. Kathleen Tillotson and Anthea Trodd), both of which use *All the Year Round* for their text.

The Woman in White was published as a volume on 15 August 1860.

No Name in *All the Year Round,* 15 March 1862–17 January 1863

Part	Date	Chapters in Volume Edition
1	15 March 1862	"The First Scene," Chapters 1, 2
2	22 March	3, 4
3	29 March	5, 6
4	5 April	7, 8
5	12 April	9
6	19 April	10
7	26 April	11, 12ᵃ
8	3 May	12 (cont.), 13ᵇ
9	10 May	13 (cont.), 14
10	17 May	15
11	24 May	"Between the Scenes"
12	31 May	"The Second Scene," Chapter 1
13	7 June	2
14	14 June	3
15	21 June	"Between the Scenes. Chronicle of Events," Sections 1–8
16	28 June	"Between the Scenes" (cont.); "The Third Scene," Chapter 1
17	5 July	2
18	12 July	3
19	19 July	4

No Name (cont.)

20	26 July	"Between the Scenes"
21	2 August	"The Fourth Scene," Chapter 1
22	9 August	2, 3
23	16 August	4
24	23 August	5
25	30 August	6
26	6 September	7
27	13 September	8
28	20 September	9
29	27 September	10
30	4 October	11, 12
31	11 October	13
32	18 October	14
33	25 October	"Between the Scenes"
34	1 November	"The Fifth Scene," Chapter 1
35	8 November	2
36	15 November	3
37	22 November	"Between the Scenes"
38	29 November	"The Sixth Scene," Chapters 1, 2; "Between the Scenes"
39	6 December	"The Seventh Scene," Chapter 1
40	13 December	2, 3
41	20 December	4[c]
42	27 December	4 (cont.); "Between the Scenes," Sections 1–4
43	3 January 1863	"Between the Scenes" (cont.); "The Last Scene," Chapter 1
44	10 January	2
45	17 January	3, 4

[a]Part 7 ends one third of the way through chapter 12 with "The servant opened the door and Mr. Pendril went in."

[b]Part 8 ends halfway through chapter 13 with "Yes: on Michael Vanstone."

[c]Part 41 ends two thirds of the way through chapter 4 with "She turned with a shriek of terror, and found herself face to face with old Mazey."

No Name was published as a volume in December 1862.

Armadale in the *Cornhill Magazine,* November 1864–June 1866

Part	Date	Chapters in Volume Edition
1	November 1864	Prologue, Chapters 1, 2, 3
2	December	Book 1, Chapter 1
3	January 1865	2, 3
4	February	4, 5
5	March	Book 2, Chapters 1, 2
6	April	3, 4
7	May	5, 6, 7
8	June	8, 9
9	July	10, 11, 12
10	August	13; Book 3, Chapters 1, 2
11	September	3, 4
12	October	5, 6, 7
13	November	8, 9
14	December	10
15	January 1866	11, 12, 13
16	February	14
17	March	15; Book 4, Chapter 1[a]
18	April	1 (cont.), 2, 3[b]
19	May	3 (cont.); Book the Last, Chapters 1, 2
20	June	3; Epilogue, Chapters 1, 2[c]

[a]Part 17 ends with the 13 October entry from "Miss Gwilt's Diary."
[b]Part 18 ends one third of the way through chapter 3 with "I instantly recognized the voice. Doctor Downward!"
[c]The appendix was not included in the serial.

Armadale was published as a volume in May 1866.

The Moonstone in *All the Year Round,* 4 January–8 August 1868

Part	Date	Chapters in Volume Edition
1	4 January 1868	Prologue, Chapters 1, 2, 3, 4; "First Period. Events Related by Gabriel Betteredge," Chapters 1, 2, 3
2	11 January	4, 5
3	18 January	6, 7

The Moonstone (cont.)

4	25 January	8, 9
5	1 February	10
6	8 February	11[a]
7	15 February	11 (cont.), 12
8	22 February	13, 14
9	29 February	15
10	7 March	16, 17
11	14 March	18, 19, 20[b]
12	21 March	20 (cont.), 21[c]
13	28 March	21 (cont.), 22
14	4 April	"Second Period. First Narrative. Miss Clack," Chapter 1
15	11 April	2
16	18 April	3, 4[d]
17	25 April	4 (cont.), 5
18	2 May	6, 7[e]
19	9 May	7 (cont.)
20	16 May	"Second Narrative. Mathew Bruff," Chapters 1, 2
21	23 May	3; "Third Narrative. Franklin Blake," Chapter 1
22	30 May	2, 3
23	6 June	4
24	13 June	5, 6
25	20 June	7
26	27 June	8
27	4 July	9
28	11 July	10
29	18 July	"Fourth Narrative. Journal of Ezra Jennings"[f]
30	25 July	"Fourth Narrative" (cont.)
31	1 August	"Fifth Narrative. Franklin Blake"
32	8 August	"Sixth Narrative. Sergeant Cuff," Chapters 1, 2, 3, 4, 5; "Seventh Narrative. Mr. Candy"; "Eighth Narrative. Gabriel Betteredge"; Epilogue, Chapters 1, 2, 3

[a]Part 6 ends two thirds through chapter 11 with the paragraph beginning "While the police officer was still pondering in solitude" and ending "out walked Rosanna Spearman."

[b]Part 11 ends one fourth through chapter 20 with the paragraph beginning "At the last conference we had held with her we had found her not overwilling to lift her eyes from the book which she had on the table."

ᶜPart 12 ends two thirds through chapter 21 with "Hot and angry as I was, the infernal confidence with which he gave me that answer closed my lips."

ᵈPart 16 ends halfway through chapter 4 with the paragraph beginning "Towards luncheon-time—not for the sake of the creature-comforts, but for the certainty of finding dear aunt—I put on my bonnet to go to Montagu Square."

ᵉPart 18 ends halfway through chapter 7 with the paragraph beginning "He led me to a chair" and ending "I can answer for that if I can answer for nothing more."

ᶠPart 29 ends with the third sentence of Ezra Jennings' journal entry for 25 June.

The Moonstone was published as a volume in July 1868.

Man and Wife in *Harper's Weekly*, 20 November 1869–6 August 1870

Chapters correspond to the edition published by P. F. Collier, New York.

Part	Date	Chapters in Volume Edition
1	20 November 1869	Prologue, Chapters 1, 2, 3, 4
2	27 November	5, 6, 7, 8, 9; "The Story," Chapters 1, 2
3	4 December	3, 4
4	11 December	5, 6
5	18 December	7, 8
6	25 December	9
7	1 January 1870	10, 11, 12ᵃ
8	8 January	12 (cont.), 13
9	15 January	14, 15, 16
10	22 January	17, 18
11	29 January	19
12	5 February	20
13	12 February	21
14	19 February	22
15	26 February	23
16	5 March	24, 25
17	12 March	26, 27
18	19 March	28, 29, 30

Man and Wife (cont.)

19	26 March	31
20	2 April	32, 33ᵇ
21	9 April	33 (cont.), 34, 35
22	16 April	36
23	23 April	37, 38ᶜ
24	30 April	38 (cont.), 39
25	7 May	40
26	14 May	41
27	21 May	42, 43
28	28 May	44
29	4 June	45
30	11 June	46ᵈ
31	18 June	46 (cont.), 47
32	25 June	48, 49
33	2 July	50, 51
34	9 July	52, 53
35	16 July	54ᵉ
36	23 July	54 (cont.), 55ᶠ
37	30 July	55 (cont.), 56, 57ᵍ
38	6 August	57 (cont.), Epilogue

ᵃPart 7 ends one fourth of the way through chapter 12 with the paragraph "In the silence which followed that discovery, a first flash of lightning passed across the window, and the low roll of thunder sounded the outbreak of the storm."

ᵇPart 20 ends one third of the way through chapter 33 with "He set forth on the road back again, to search among the company at the lake for Mrs. Glenarm."

ᶜPart 23 ends one third of the way through chapter 38 with the paragraph beginning "Sir Patrick handed the newspaper silently to Arnold."

ᵈPart 30 ends halfway through chapter 46 with "Lady Lundie yielded, and returned to her place. They all waited in silence for the opening of the doors."

ᵉPart 35 ends in section 10 of "The Manuscript," the last paragraph beginning "I have reason for keeping silence here."

ᶠPart 36 ends two thirds of the way through chapter 55 with the paragraph beginning "Geoffrey ran upstairs" and ending "The bedcurtains, nevertheless, were in a blaze of fire."

ᵍPart 37 ends two thirds of the way through chapter 57 with the paragraph beginning "She entered the room" and ending "In less than five minutes, she was in a deep sleep."

Man and Wife in Cassell's Magazine, December 1869–September 1870

Cassell's Magazine was published weekly between 2 May 1868 and 7 November 1874. Because the only run I have been able to examine, the one at the British Library, is bound in monthly, not weekly, covers, I am able to indicate the content by months only for this novel and the following one. Chapters correspond to the Tauchnitz edition, Leipzig, 1870.

Part	Date	Chapters in Volume Edition
1	December 1869	Prologue, Chapters 1, 2, 3, 4, 5, 6, 7, 8, 9; "The Story," Chapters 1, 2, 3, 4, 5, 6
2	January 1870	7, 8, 9, 10, 11, 12, 13
3	February	14, 15, 16, 17, 18, 19, 20, 21
4	March	22, 23, 24, 25, 26, 27, 28, 29
5	April	30, 31, 32, 33, 34, 35, 36, 37[a]
6	May	37 (cont.), 38, 39, 40, 41, 42, 43, 44
7	June	45, 46, 47, 48, 49
8	July	50, 51, 52, 53, 54
9	August	55, 56, 57, 58, 59, 60[b]
10	September	60 (cont.), 61, 62, Epilogue

[a]Part 5 ends fifteen paragraphs into chapter 37 with "He set forth on his road back again, to search among the company at the lake, for Mrs. Glenarm."

[b]Part 9 ends two thirds of the way through chapter 60 with the paragraph beginning "Geoffrey ran upstairs" and concluding "The bedcurtains, nevertheless, were in a blaze of fire."

Man and Wife was published as a volume in June 1870.

Poor Miss Finch in Cassell's Magazine, October 1871–March 1872

See the note on serialization of Man and Wife in Cassell's.

Part	Date	Chapters in Volume Edition
1	October 1871	1, 2, 3, 4, 5, 6, 7, 8, 9, 10, 11, 12, 13
2	November	14, 15, 16, 17, 18, 19, 20, 21, 22, 23, 24, 25
3	December	26, 27, 28, 29, 30, 31, 32
4	January 1872	33, 34, 35, 36, 37
5	February	38, 39, 40, 41, 42, 43
6	March	44, 45, 46, 47, 48, 49, Epilogue

Poor Miss Finch was published as a volume on 26 January 1872.

The New Magdalen in Temple Bar, October 1872–July 1873

Part	Date	Chapters in Volume Edition
1	October 1872	1, 2, 3, 4, 5
2	November	6, 7, 8
3	December	9, 10, 11
4	January 1873	12, 13, 14, 15
5	February	16, 17, 18, 19
6	March	20, 21
7	April	22, 23
8	May	24, 25, 26, 27[a]
9	June	27 (cont.), 28, 29
10	July	Epilogue

[a]The part ends twenty-two paragraphs short of the chapter; the last paragraph commences "A few minutes had been all she asked for."

The New Magdalen was published as a volume on 17 May 1873.

The Law and the Lady in the Graphic, 26 September 1874–13 March 1875

Part	Date	Chapters in Volume Edition
1	26 September 1874	1, 2, 3
2	3 October	4, 5, 6
3	10 October	7, 8
4	17 October	9, 10[a]
5	24 October	10 (cont.)
6	31 October	11, 12
7	7 November	13, 14
8	14 November	15, 16
9	21 November	17, 18[b]
10	28 November	18 (cont.), 19
11	5 December	20, 21
12	12 December	22, 23, 24[c]
13	19 December	24 (cont.), 25

The Law and the Lady (cont.)

14	26 December	26, 27
15	2 January 1875	28, 29
16	9 January	30, 31
17	16 January	32, 33
18	23 January	34, 35
19	30 January	36, 37
20	6 February	38, 39, 40[d]
21	13 February	40 (cont.)
22	20 February	41, 42
23	27 February	43, 44, 45
24	6 March	46, 47, 48[e]
25	13 March	48 (cont.), 49, 50

[a]Part 4 ends one fifth of the way through chapter 10 with the paragraph beginning "His eyes, after meeting mine, travelled downwards to my foot."

[b]Part 9 concludes one third of the way through chapter 18 with the paragraph beginning "On the return of the judges into the court" and concluding "The reading of the extracts from the letters and the extracts from the Diary began."

[c]Part 12 ends halfway through chapter 24 with " 'Follow me,' said Mrs. Macallan, mounting the stairs in the dark. 'I know where to find him.' "

[d]Part 20 concludes one third of the way through chapter 40 with "We all waited to see what he would do, to hear what he would say, next."

[e]Part 24 ends one third of the way through chapter 48 with " 'I have had a letter, too, this morning,' he said, 'And *I*, Valeria, have no secrets from *you*.' "

The Law and the Lady was published as a volume in February 1875.

The Two Destinies in *Temple Bar,* January–September 1876

Part	Date	Chapters in Volume Edition
1	January 1876	Prelude, 1, 2, 3, 4[a]
2	February	Book 1, Chapters 1, 2, 3, 4
3	March	5, 6, 7, 8, 9[b]
4	April	9 (cont.), 10, 11, 12, 13, 14
5	May	Book 2, Chapters 1, 2, 3[c]
6	June	4, 5, 6

The Two Destinies (cont.)

7	July	7, 8, 9, 10, 11
8	August	12, 13, 14, 15, 16
9	September	17, 18, 19, 20, Finale

ªIn the serial, the chapters do not renumber after the prelude.

ᵇPart 3 contains only the first sixteen paragraphs, ending with "The curtain rose for the ballet, I made the best excuse I could to my friends, and instantly left the box."

ᶜPart 5 concludes with the note, "A sudden attack of illness has prevented the author from proceeding farther with the Number of 'The Two Destinies,' published this month. He has every hope of being able to continue the Story next month in a Number of the customary length." The part is thirteen pages long; the previous parts varied from twenty-three to twenty-six pages.

The Two Destinies was published as a volume in September 1876.

The Haunted Hotel in *Belgravia,* June–November 1878

Part	Date	Chapters in Volume Edition
1	June 1878	1, 2, 3, 4, 5
2	July	6, 7, 8, 9, 10
3	August	11, 12, 13, 14, 15
4	September	16, 17, 18, 19, 20
5	October	21, 22, 23, 24, 25
6	November	26, 27, 28, Postscript

The Haunted Hotel was published as a volume in November 1878.

Fallen Leaves in the *World,* 1 January–23 July 1879

Part	Date	Chapters in Volume Edition
1	1 January 1879	Prologue, Chapters 1, 2, 3, 4, 5
2	8 January	6; "The Story," Book 1, Chapter 1
3	15 January	2, 3

Fallen Leaves (cont.)

4	22 January	4, 5
5	29 January	Book 2, Chapter 1[a]
6	5 February	1 (cont.), 2
7	12 February	Book 3, Chapter 1
8	19 February	2
9	26 February	3, 4
10	5 March	Book 4, Chapter 1
11	12 March	2, 3
12	19 March	4
13	26 March	Book 5, Chapters 1, 2
14	2 April	3
15	9 April	4, 5[b]
16	16 April	5 (cont.), 6; Book 6, Chapter 1[c]
17	23 April	1 (cont.), 2
18	30 April	3
19	7 May	4, 5
20	14 May	6; Book 7, Chapter 1[d]
21	21 May	1 (cont.), 2
22	28 May	3, 4
23	4 June	5, 6[e]
24	11 June	6 (cont.); Book 8, Chapter 1
25	18 June	2, 3
26	25 June	4, 5[f]
27	2 July	5 (cont.), 6
28	9 July	7, 8
29	16 July	9, 10
30	23 July	11, 12

[a]Part 5 ends halfway through the chapter with the question "Was she having a peep at the young Socialist?"

[b]Part 15 ends halfway through the chapter with "Put on your bonnet, and wait till we are out in the street."

[c]Only the first eighteen paragraphs of the chapter are included in part 16, the last commencing "Some of the nearest drinkers at the bar looked round laughing."

[d]Part 20 ends halfway through the chapter with the sentence "While you are a Socialist, you are a stranger to me."

[e]Part 23 ends halfway through the chapter, the last paragraph beginning "Amelius told Sally to wait in the cab."

[f]Part 26 includes only the first twenty-three paragraphs of the chapter. The installment concludes with "Give me my lesson, Amelius! please give me my lesson!"

Fallen Leaves was published as a volume in July 1879.

Fallen Leaves in *Canadian Monthly,* February 1879–March 1880

Part	Date	Chapters in Volume Edition
1	February 1879	Prologue, 1, 2, 3, 4, 5, 6; Book 1, Chapter 1
2	March	2, 3, 4, 5
3	April	Book 2, Chapter 1[a]
4	May	1 (cont.), 2; Book 3, Chapter 1
5	June	2, 3, 4
6	July	Book 4, Chapters 1, 2, 3
7	August	4; Book 5, Chapters 1, 2, 3[b]
8	September	3 (cont.), 4, 5, 6; Book 6, Chapter 1[c]
9	October	1 (cont.), 2, 3
10	November	4, 5, 6
11	December	Book 7, Chapters 1, 2, 3, 4
12	January 1880	5, 6; Book 8, Chapter 1
13	February	2, 3, 4, 5
14	March	6, 7, 8, 9, 10, 11, 12

[a]Part 3 ends halfway through the chapter with the question "Was she having a peep at the young Socialist?"
[b]Part 7 ends thirty paragraphs from the end of the chapter with "There Amelius paused, and took his first drink of water."
[c]Only the first two paragraphs of the chapter are included.

The Black Robe in *Canadian Monthly,* November 1880–June 1881

Part	Date	Chapters in Volume Edition
1	November 1880	"Before the Story," Chapters 1, 2, 3, 4, 5, 6, 7, 8, 9, 10; "The Story," Book 1, Chapter 1
2	December	2, 3, 4, 5, 6, 7
3	January 1881	8, 9, 10, 11, 12[a]
4	February	12 (cont.), 13; Book 2, Chapters 1, 2, 3, 4; Book 3, Chapters 1, 2, 3
5	March	4, 5; Book 4, Chapter 1
6	April	2, 3, 4, 5, 6, 7, 8
7	May	Book 5, Chapters 1, 2, 3, 4; "After the Story," 1[b]
8	June	1 (cont.)

ªPart 3 ends twenty-five paragraphs short of the end of the chapter with "She was not naturally timid. What did it mean?"

ᵇPart 7 ends toward the close of the 29 January entry with "In the morning the lock was found broken, and the papers and the boy missing together."

The Black Robe was published as a volume in April 1881.

Heart and Science in *Belgravia,* August 1882–June 1883

Part	Date	Chapters in Volume Edition
1	August 1882	1, 2, 3, 4, 5, 6
2	September	7, 8, 9, 10
3	October	11, 12, 13, 14, 15
4	November	16, 17, 18, 19, 20
5	December	21, 22, 23, 24, 25, 26
6	January 1883	27, 28, 29, 30, 31, 32
7	February	33, 34, 35, 36, 37, 38
8	March	39, 40, 41, 42, 43, 44, 45
9	April	46, 47, 48, 49, 50, 51
10	May	52, 53, 54, 55, 56, 57, 58, 59
11	June	60, 61, 62, 63

Heart and Science was published as a volume in April 1883.

The Evil Genius in the *Leigh Journal and Times,* 11 December 1885–30 April 1886

Part	Date	Chapters in Volume Edition
1	11 December 1885	"Before the Story," Chapters, 1, 2, 3
2	18 December	4, 5, 6, 7, 8, 9
3	25 December	10; "The Story," Chapters 1, 2, 3, 4

The Evil Genius (cont.)

4	31 December	5, 6, 7, 8, 9
5	8 January 1886	10, 11, 12, 13
6	15 January	14, 15, 16, 17, 18, 19
7	22 January	20, 21, 22, 23, 24, 25
8	29 January	26, 27
9	5 February	28, 29
10	12 February	30, 31
11	19 February	32, 33
12	26 February	34, 35
13	5 March	36, 37
14	12 March	38, 39, 40
15	19 March	41, 42
16	26 March	43, 44
17	2 April	45, 46
18	9 April	47, 48
19	16 April	49, 50, 51
20	23 April	52, 53, 54
21	30 April	55; "After the Story," Chapters 1, 2, 3

The Evil Genius was published as a volume in September 1886.

Blind Love in the Illustrated London News, 6 July–28 December 1889

Part	Date	Chapters in Volume Edition
1	6 July 1889	Prologue, Chapters 1, 2, 3, 4, 5
2	13 July	6, 7, 8, 9
3	20 July	10, 11; "The Story," Chapter 1
4	27 July	2, 3, 4[a]
5	3 August	4 (cont.), 5, 6
6	10 August	7, 8
7	17 August	9, 10, 11
8	24 August	12, 13
9	31 August	14, 15, 16, 17
10	7 September	18, 19, 20

Blind Love (cont.)

11	14 September	21, 22, 23
12	21 September	24, 25, 26
13	28 September	27, 28, 29, 30
14	5 October	31, 32, 33
15	12 October	34, 35, 36
16	19 October	37, 38, 39
17	26 October	40, 41, 42
18	2 November	43, 44, 45, 46
19	9 November	47, 48, 49[b]
20	16 November	50, 51
21	23 November	52, 53, 54
22	30 November	55
23	7 December	56, 57, 58
24	14 December	59, 60
25	21 December	61, 62
26	28 December	63, 64, Epilogue

[a]Part 4 ends halfway through chapter 4 with the paragraph beginning "Mountjoy had his reasons for wishing to see the husband."

[b]Wilkie Collins had died on 23 September. He had completed through chapter 48. Sir Walter Besant completed the novel (chapter 49–epilogue) using a synopsis drawn up by Collins.

The volume edition was published in January 1890.

Charles Dickens (1812–70)

Pickwick Papers, **twenty parts in nineteen monthly installments, April 1836–November 1837**

Part	Date	Chapters in Volume Edition
1	April 1836	1, 2, 3[a]
2	May	3 (cont.), 4, 5
3	June	6, 7, 8
4	July	9, 10, 11
5	August	12, 13, 14
6	September	15, 16, 17
7	October	18, 19, 20
8	November	21, 22, 23
9	December	24, 25, 26
10	January 1837	27, 28, 29
11	February	30, 31, 32
12	March	33, 34
13	April	35, 36, 37
14	May[b]	38, 39, 40
15	July	41, 42, 43
16	August	44, 45, 46
17	September	47, 48, 49
18	October	50, 51, 52
19–20	November	53, 54, 55, 56, 57

[a]Part 2 began with "The Stroller's Tale."
[b]There was no issue in June because of the death of Dickens' sister-in-law, Mary Hogarth, on 7 May 1837.

The Penguin edition (ed. Robert Patten) uses asterisks in the text to mark the end of serial parts; also, the table of contents lists part numbers with Roman numerals.

Pickwick Papers was also published in five parts in Philadelphia in 1836–37 by Carey, Lea, and Blanchard; in twenty-six parts in New York in 1837–38 by James Turney; and in twenty parts in Calcutta in 1837–38 by William Rushton. The novel was published as a volume on 17 November 1837.

Oliver Twist in *Bentley's Miscellany*, February 1837–April 1839

Part	Date	Chapters in Volume Edition
1	February 1837	1, 2
2	March	3, 4
3	April	5, 6
4	May	7, 8
5	July[a]	9, 10, 11
6	August	12, 13
7	September	14, 15
8	November[b]	16, 17
9	December	18, 19
10	January 1838	20, 21, 22
11	February	23, 24, 25
12	March	26, 27
13	April	28, 29, 30
14	May	31, 32
15	June	33, 34
16	July	35, 36, 37
17	August	38, 39
18	October[c]	40, 41
19	November	42, 43
20	December	44, 45
21	January 1839	46, 47, 48, 49[d]
22	February	49 (cont.), 50, 51[e]
23	March	51 (cont.)
24	April	52, 53

[a]There was no installment in the June issue of *Bentley's Miscellany* because of the death of Dickens' sister-in-law, Mary Hogarth, on 7 May 1837.

[b]In the October issue there was no installment of *Oliver Twist*; instead, Dickens published the "Full Report of the First Meeting of the Mudfog Association for the Advancement of Everything."

[c]Instead of an installment of *Oliver Twist*, the September 1838 issue contains the "Full Report of the Second Meeting of the Mudfog Association for the Advancement of Everything."

[d]Part 21 ended one third of the way through chapter 49 with "The end of a year found him contracted, solemnly contracted, to that daughter; the object of the first, true, ardent, only passion of a guileless, untried girl."

[e]Part 22 ended one fourth of the way through chapter 51 with " 'This child,' said Mr. Brownlow, drawing Oliver to him, and laying his hand upon his head, 'is your half-brother; the illegitimate son of your father, my dear friend Edwin Leeford, by poor young Agnes Fleming, who died in giving him birth.' "

The Clarendon edition (ed. Kathleen Tillotson, 1966) identifies the serial parts. The novel was published as three volumes on 9 November 1838. It was reprinted in monthly parts between 31 December 1845 and 30 September 1846.

Nicholas Nickleby, twenty parts in nineteen monthly installments, April 1838–October 1839

Part	Date	Chapters in Volume Edition
1	April 1838	1, 2, 3, 4
2	May	5, 6, 7
3	June	8, 9, 10
4	July	11, 12, 13, 14
5	August	15, 16, 17
6	September	18, 19, 20
7	October	21, 22, 23
8	November	24, 25, 26
9	December	27, 28, 29
10	January 1839	30, 31, 32, 33
11	February	34, 35, 36
12	March	37, 38, 39
13	April	40, 41, 42
14	May	43, 44, 45
15	June	46, 47, 48
16	July	49, 50, 51
17	August	52, 53, 54
18	September	55, 56, 57, 58
19–20	October	59, 60, 61, 62, 63, 64, 65

The Scolar Press published a facsimile edition of the serial parts (ed. Michael Slater, 1972). The Penguin edition (ed. Slater) uses asterisks in the text and Roman numerals on the contents page to identify the serial parts. The novel was published as a volume on 23 October 1839. It was also published in twenty parts in nineteen installments in Philadelphia in 1838–39 by Lea and Blanchard.

The Old Curiosity Shop in *Master Humphrey's Clock*, 25 April 1840–6 February 1841

Part	Date	Chapters in Volume Edition
1	25 April 1840	1
2	16 May	2
3	23 May	3, 4
4	30 May	5
5	6 June	6, 7
6	13 June	8
7	20 June	9, 10
8	27 June	11, 12
9	4 July	13, 14
10	11 July	15, 16
11	18 July	17, 18
12	25 July	19, 20
13	1 August	21, 22
14	8 August	23, 24
15	15 August	25, 26
16	22 August	27, 28
17	29 August	29, 30
18	5 September	31, 32
19	12 September	33, 34
20	19 September	35, 36
21	26 September	37
22	3 October	38, 39
23	10 October	40, 41
24	17 October	42, 43
25	24 October	44, 45
26	31 October	46, 47
27	7 November	48, 49
28	14 November	50, 51
29	21 November	52, 53
30	28 November	54, 55
31	5 December	56, 57
32	12 December	58, 59
33	19 December	60, 61
34	26 December	62, 63
35	2 January 1841	64, 65
36	9 January	66

The Old Curiosity Shop (cont.)

37	16 January	67, 68
38	23 January	69, 70
39	30 January	71, 72
40	6 February	Chapter the Last

The Penguin edition (ed. Angus Easson) lists the serial parts in "A Note on the Text"; also, asterisks mark the end of each serial part.

Barnaby Rudge in *Master Humphrey's Clock*, 13 February–27 November 1841

Part	Date	Chapters in Volume Edition
1	13 February 1841	1
2	20 February	2, 3
3	27 February	4, 5
4	6 March	6, 7
5	13 March	8, 9
6	20 March	10, 11
7	27 March	12
8	3 April	13, 14
9	10 April	15, 16
10	17 April	17, 18
11	24 April	19, 20
12	1 May	21, 22
13	8 May	23, 24
14	15 May	25, 26
15	22 May	27, 28
16	29 May	29, 30
17	5 June	31, 32
18	12 June	33, 34
19	19 June	35, 36
20	26 June	37, 38
21	3 July	39, 40
22	10 July	41, 42
23	17 July	43, 44

Barnaby Rudge (cont.)

24	24 July	45, 46
25	31 July	47, 48
26	7 August	49, 50
27	14 August	51, 52
28	21 August	53, 54
29	28 August	55, 56
30	4 September	57, 58
31	11 September	59, 60
32	18 September	61, 62
33	25 September	63, 64
34	2 October	65, 66
35	9 October	67, 68
36	16 October	69, 70
37	23 October	71, 72
38	30 October	73, 74
39	6 November	75, 76
40	13 November	77, 78
41	20 November	79, 80
42	27 November	81, Chapter the Last

The Penguin edition (ed. G. W. Spence) identifies the serial parts.
Barnaby Rudge was also published in eight monthly parts in Leipzig in 1841 by J. J. Weber.

Martin Chuzzlewit, twenty parts in nineteen monthly installments, January 1843–July 1844

Part	Date	Chapters in Volume Edition
1	January 1843	1, 2, 3
2	February	4, 5
3	March	6, 7, 8
4	April	9, 10
5	May	11, 12
6	June	13, 14, 15
7	July	16, 17

Martin Chuzzlewit (cont.)

8	August	18, 19, 20
9	September	21, 22, 23
10	October	24, 25, 26
11	November	27, 28, 29
12	December	30, 31, 32
13	January 1844	33, 34, 35
14	February	36, 37, 38
15	March	39, 40, 41
16	April	42, 43, 44
17	May	45, 46, 47
18	June	48, 49, 50
19–20	July	51, 52, 53, 54

The Penguin edition (ed. P. N. Furbank) identifies the serial parts.

Martin Chuzzlewit was also published in seven parts in New York in 1844 by Harper and Brothers. The novel was published as a volume on 16 July 1844.

Dombey and Son, twenty parts in nineteen monthly installments, October 1846–April 1848

Part	Date	Chapters in Volume Edition
1	October 1846	1, 2, 3, 4
2	November	5, 6, 7
3	December	8, 9, 10
4	January 1847	11, 12, 13
5	February	14, 15, 16
6	March	17, 18, 19
7	April	20, 21, 22
8	May	23, 24, 25
9	June	26, 27, 28
10	July	29, 30, 31
11	August	32, 33, 34
12	September	35, 36, 37, 38
13	October	39, 40, 41
14	November	42, 43, 44, 45

Dombey and Son (cont.)

15	December	46, 47, 48
16	January 1848	49, 50, 51
17	February	52, 53, 54
18	March	55, 56, 57
19–20	April	58, 59, 60, 61, 62

The Clarendon edition (ed. Alan Horsman, 1974) identifies the serial parts. *Dombey and Son* was also published in twenty parts in nineteen monthly installments in 1847–48 in New York by Wiley and Putnam, and in 1846–48 in Boston by Bradbury and Guild. The novel was published as a volume on 12 April 1848.

David Copperfield, twenty parts in nineteen monthly installments, May 1849–November 1850

Part	Date	Chapters in Volume Edition
1	May 1849	1, 2, 3
2	June	4, 5, 6
3	July	7, 8, 9
4	August	10, 11, 12
5	September	13, 14, 15
6	October	16, 17, 18
7	November	19, 20, 21
8	December	22, 23, 24
9	January 1850	25, 26, 27
10	February	28, 29, 30, 31
11	March	32, 33, 34
12	April	35, 36, 37
13	May	38, 39, 40
14	June	41, 42, 43
15	July	44, 45, 46
16	August	47, 48, 49, 50
17	September	51, 52, 53
18	October	54, 55, 56, 57
19–20	November	58, 59, 60, 61, 62, 63, 64

The Clarendon edition (ed. Nina Burgis) and the Penguin edition (ed. Trevor Blunt) both identify the serial parts.

David Copperfield was also published in twenty parts in nineteen monthly installments in 1849–50 in New York, eleven parts by John Wiley, nine by G. P. Putnam; and in Philadelphia by Lea and Blanchard. The novel was published as a volume on 15 November 1850.

Bleak House, twenty parts in nineteen monthly installments, March 1852–September 1853

Part	Date	Chapters in Volume Edition
1	March 1852	1, 2, 3, 4
2	April	5, 6, 7
3	May	8, 9, 10
4	June	11, 12, 13
5	July	14, 15, 16
6	August	17, 18, 19
7	September	20, 21, 22
8	October	23, 24, 25
9	November	26, 27, 28, 29
10	December	30, 31, 32
11	January 1853	33, 34, 35
12	February	36, 37, 38
13	March	39, 40, 41, 42
14	April	43, 44, 45, 46
15	May	47, 48, 49
16	June	50, 51, 52, 53
17	July	54, 55, 56
18	August	57, 58, 59
19–20	September	60, 61, 62, 63, 64, 65, 66, 67

The Crowell edition (ed. Duane Devries), the Norton Critical Edition (ed. George Ford and Sylvère Monod), and the Penguin edition (ed. Norman Page) all identify the serial parts.

Bleak House was also published in twenty parts in nineteen monthly installments in 1852–53 in New York by Harper and Brothers.

Hard Times in *Household Words*, 1 April–12 August 1854

Part	Date	Chapters in Volume Edition
1	1 April 1854	1, 2, 3
2	8 April	4, 5
3	15 April	6
4	22 April	7, 8
5	29 April	9, 10
6	6 May	11, 12
7	13 May	13, 14
8	20 May	15, 16
9	27 May	17
10	3 June	18, 19
11	10 June	20, 21
12	17 June	22
13	24 June	23
14	1 July	24
15	8 July	25, 26
16	15 July	27, 28
17	22 July	29, 30
18	29 July	31, 32
19	5 August	33, 34
20	12 August	35, 36, 37

The Norton Critical Edition (ed. George Ford and Sylvère Monod) identifies the serial parts.

Little Dorrit, twenty parts in nineteen monthly installments, December 1855–June 1857

Part	Date	Chapters in Volume Edition
1	December 1855	Book 1, Chapters 1, 2, 3, 4
2	January 1856	5, 6, 7, 8
3	February	9, 10, 11
4	March	12, 13, 14
5	April	15, 16, 17, 18
6	May	19, 20, 21, 22

Little Dorrit (cont.)

7	June	23, 24, 25
8	July	26, 27, 28, 29
9	August	30, 31, 32
10	September	33, 34, 35, 36
11	October	Book 2, Chapters 1, 2, 3, 4
12	November	5, 6, 7
13	December	8, 9, 10, 11
14	January 1857	12, 13, 14
15	February	15, 16, 17, 18
16	March	19, 20, 21, 22
17	April	23, 24, 25, 26
18	May	27, 28, 29
19–20	June	30, 31, 32, 33, 34

The Penguin edition (ed. John Holloway) identifies the serial parts; in the copy I examined the asterisk that ought to appear after book 2, chapter 29, marking the break between parts 18 and 19–20, is missing. The Clarendon edition (ed. H. P. Sucksmith) and the Odyssey edition also identify the serial parts.

Little Dorrit was published as a volume on 30 May 1857.

A Tale of Two Cities in *All the Year Round,* 30 April–26 November 1859

Part	Date	Chapters in Volume Edition
1	30 April 1859	Book 1, Chapters 1, 2, 3
2	7 May	4
3	14 May	5
4	21 May	6
5	28 May	Book 2, Chapters 1, 2
6	4 June	3
7	11 June	4, 5
8	18 June	6
9	25 June	7, 8
10	2 July	9
11	9 July	10, 11

A Tale of Two Cities (cont.)

12	16 July	12, 13
13	23 July	14
14	30 July	15
15	6 August	16
16	13 August	17, 18
17	20 August	19, 20
18	27 August	21
19	3 September	22, 23
20	10 September	24
21	17 September	Book 3, Chapter 1
22	24 September	2, 3
23	1 October	4, 5
24	8 October	6, 7
25	15 October	8
26	22 October	9
27	29 October	10
28	5 November	11, 12
29	12 November	13
30	19 November	14
31	26 November	15

A Tale of Two Cities was also published in eight parts in seven monthly installments in 1859 in London by Chapman and Hall.

Great Expectations in *All the Year Round,* 1 December 1860–3 August 1861

Part	Date	Chapters in Volume Edition
1	1 December 1860	1, 2
2	8 December	3, 4
3	15 December	5
4	22 December	6, 7
5	29 December	8

Great Expectations (cont.)

6	5 January 1861	9, 10
7	12 January	11
8	19 January	12, 13
9	26 January	14, 15
10	2 February	16, 17
11	9 February	18
12	16 February	19
13	23 February	20, 21
14	2 March	22
15	9 March	23, 24
16	16 March	25, 26
17	23 March	27, 28
18	30 March	29
19	6 April	30, 31
20	13 April	32, 33
21	20 April	34, 35
22	27 April	36, 37
23	4 May	38
24	11 May	39
25	18 May	40
26	25 May	41, 42
27	1 June	43, 44
28	8 June	45, 46
29	15 June	47, 48
30	22 June	49, 50
31	29 June	51, 52
32	6 July	53
33	13 July	54
34	20 July	55, 56
35	27 July	57
36	3 August	58, 59

The Macmillan edition (ed. R. D. McMaster) and the Penguin edition (ed. Angus Calder) identify the serial parts.

Our Mutual Friend, twenty parts in nineteen monthly installments, May 1864–November 1865

Part	Date	Chapters in Volume Edition
1	May 1864	Book 1, Chapters 1, 2, 3, 4
2	June	5, 6, 7
3	July	8, 9, 10
4	August	11, 12, 13
5	September	14, 15, 16, 17
6	October	Book 2, Chapters 1, 2, 3
7	November	4, 5, 6
8	December	7, 8, 9, 10
9	January 1865	11, 12, 13
10	February	14, 15, 16
11	March	Book 3, Chapters 1, 2, 3, 4
12	April	5, 6, 7
13	May	8, 9, 10
14	June	11, 12, 13, 14
15	July	15, 16, 17
16	August	Book 4, Chapters 1, 2, 3, 4
17	September	5, 6, 7
18	October	8, 9, 10, 11
19–20	November	12, 13, 14, 15, 16, 17

The Mystery of Edwin Drood in monthly shilling parts,ᵃ April–September 1870

Part	Date	Chapters in Volume Edition
1	April 1870	1, 2, 3, 4, 5
2	May	6, 7, 8, 9
3	June	10, 11, 12
4	July	13, 14, 15, 16
5	August	17, 18, 19, 20
6	September	21, 22, 23

ᵃTwelve parts were projected. Dickens died after the publication of part 3.

The Clarendon edition (ed. Margaret Caldwell, 1972) identifies the serial parts. The Penguin edition (ed. Arthur J. Cox, 1974) reprints Dickens' number plans and notes for the novel.

George Eliot (Mary Ann Evans) (1819–80)

Romola in the *Cornhill Magazine,* July 1862–August 1863

Part	Date	Chapters in Volume Edition
1	July 1862	Proem, Chapters 1, 2, 3, 4, 5
2	August	6, 7, 8, 9, 10
3	September	11, 12, 13, 14
4	October	15, 16, 17, 18, 19, 20
5	November	21, 22, 23, 24, 25, 26
6	December	27, 28, 29, 30, 31, 32
7	January 1863	33, 34, 35, 36, 37
8	February	38, 39, 40, 41
9	March	42, 43, 44, 45, 46
10	April	47, 48, 49, 50, 51
11	May	52, 53, 54, 55, 56
12	June	57, 58, 59, 60, 61
13	July	62, 63, 64, 65, 66, 67
14	August	68, 69, 70, 71, 72, Epilogue

Middlemarch in eight parts, December 1871–December 1872

Part	Date	Chapters in Volume Edition
1	December 1871	Book 1
2	February 1872	Book 2
3	April	Book 3
4	June	Book 4
5	August	Book 5
6	October	Book 6
7	November	Book 7
8	December	Book 8

Daniel Deronda in eight parts, February–September 1876

Part	Date	Chapters in Volume Edition
1	February 1876	Book 1
2	March	Book 2
3	April	Book 3
4	May	Book 4
5	June	Book 5
6	July	Book 6
7	August	Book 7
8	September	Book 8

Elizabeth Gaskell (1810–65)

Cranford in *Household Words,* 13 December 1851–21 May 1853

Part	Date	Chapters in Volume Edition
1	13 December 1851	1, 2
2	3 January 1852	3, 4
3	13 March	5, 6
4	3 April	7, 8
5	8 January 1853	9, 10ᵃ
6	15 January	10 (cont.), 11
7	2 April	12, 13
8	7 May	14
9	21 May	15, 16

ᵃPart 5 ends halfway through chapter 10 with the paragraph beginning "Lady Glenmire (who had evidently taken very kindly to Cranford) did not like the idea of Mrs. Jamieson's going to Cheltenham."

The edition of *Cranford* (ed. Elizabeth Porges Watson, 1972) in the Oxford English Novels series collates the *Household Words* text with the first book edition of 1853 and also with the 1855 and 1864 editions.

North and South in *Household Words*, 2 September 1854–27 January 1855

Part	Date	Chapters in Volume Edition
1	2 September 1854	1, 2
2	9 September	3, 4
3	16 September	5
4	23 September	6, 7
5	30 September	8, 9
6	7 October	10, 11
7	14 October	12, 13
8	21 October	14, 15
9	28 October	16, 17
10	4 November	18, 19
11	11 November	20, 21
12	18 November	22, 23
13	25 November	24, 25, 26
14	2 December	27, 28
15	9 December	29, 30
16	16 December	31, 32, 33
17	23 December	34, 35
18	30 December	36, 37
19	6 January 1855	38, 39
20	13 January	40, 41
21	20 January	42, 43, 44[a]
22	27 January	49, 51, 52

[a]Chapter 44 was rewritten after serialization. Also, note that chapters 45, 46, 47, 48, and 50 were added for the volume edition.

North and South was published as a volume in March 1855.

The introduction to *North and South* (ed. Angus Easson, 1973) in the Oxford English Novels series gives a brief account of the problems of serialization.

My Lady Lιdlow in *Household Words*, 19 June–25 September 1858

Part	Date	Chapters in Volume Edition
1	19 June 1858	1
2	26 June	2
3	3 July	3
4	10 July	4
5	17 July	5
6	24 July	6
7	31 July	7
8	7 August	8
9	14 August	9
10	28 August	10
11	4 September	11
12	11 September	12
13	18 September	13
14	25 September	14[a]

[a]The final two paragraphs in the volume edition were not included in the serial.

My Lady Ludlow was published as a volume in March 1859.

Cousin Phillis in the *Cornhill Magazine,* November 1863–February 1864

Part	Date	Parts in Volume Edition
1	November 1863	Part 1
2	December	Part 2
3	January 1864	Part 3
4	February	Part 4

Cousin Phillis was published as a volume in December 1865.

Wives and Daughters in the *Cornhill Magazine,* August 1864–January 1866

Part	Date	Chapters in Volume Edition
1	August 1864	1, 2, 3
2	September	4ᵃ, 5, 6
3	October	7, 8, 9
4	November	10, 11
5	December	12, 13, 14
6	January 1865	15, 16, 17
7	February	18, 19, 20
8	March	21, 22, 23
9	April	24, 25, 26
10	May	27, 28, 29
11	June	30, 31, 32
12	July	33, 34, 35, 36
13	August	37, 38, 39, 40
14	September	41, 42, 43, 44, 45
15	October	46, 47, 48, 49, 50
16	November	51, 52ᵇ, 53, 54
17	December	55, 56, 57, 58, 59
18	January 1866	60ᶜ

ᵃIn the serial the first twelve paragraphs of the present chapter 5 were included in chapter 4.

ᵇIn the serial the first fourteen paragraphs of chapter 52 were in chapter 51.

ᶜThe last installment was completed by Frederick Greenwood. Elizabeth Gaskell had died on 12 November 1865.

Wives and Daughters was published as a volume in February 1866.

The Penguin edition (ed. Frank Glover Smith, 1969) claims to be based on the serial version in the *Cornhill*. Angus Easson in a letter to the *Times Literary Supplement* (14 June 1974, p. 641) refutes this assertion.

Thomas Hardy (1840–1928)

A Pair of Blue Eyes in *Tinsley's Magazine,* September 1872–July 1873

Part	Date	Chapters in Volume Edition
1	September 1872	1ª, 2, 3, 4, 5
2	October	6, 7, 8
3	November	9, 10, 11
4	December	12, 13, 14
5	January 1873	15, 16, 17, 18
6	February	19, 20, 21
7	March	22, 23, 24, 25
8	April	26, 27, 28
9	May	29, 30, 31
10	June	32, 33, 34, 35, 36
11	July	37, 38, 39, 40

ªChapter 1 was rewritten and reduced for the volume edition.

A Pair of Blue Eyes was published as a volume at the end of May 1873.

Far from the Madding Crowd in the *Cornhill Magazine,* January–December 1874

Part	Date	Chapters in Volume Edition
1	January 1874	1, 2, 3, 4, 5
2	February	6, 7, 8
3	March	9, 10, 11, 12, 13, 14
4	April	15, 16, 17, 18, 19, 20
5	May	21, 22, 23, 24
6	June	25, 26, 27, 28, 29
7	July	30, 31, 32, 33
8	August	34, 35, 36, 37, 38

Far from the Madding Crowd (cont.)

9	September	39, 40, 41, 42
10	October	43, 44, 45, 46, 47
11	November	48, 49, 50, 51
12	December	52, 53, 54, 55, 56, 57

The novel was also published serially in the United States in *Every Saturday, Littell's Living Age,* the *Eclectic Magazine,* and the *Semi-Weekly New York Tribune.*
Far from the Madding Crowd was published as a volume on 23 November 1874.

The Hand of Ethelberta in the *Cornhill Magazine,* July 1875–May 1876

Part	Date	Chapters in Volume Edition
1	July 1875	1, 2, 3, 4
2	August	5, 6, 7, 8[a]
3	September	9, 10, 11[b], 12, 13
4	October	14, 15, 16, 17, 18, 19
5	November	20, 21, 22, 23, 24
6	December	25, 26, 27, 28
7	January 1876	29, 30, 31, 32[c]
8	February	33, 34, 35, 36
9	March	37, 38, 39, 40
10	April	41, 42, 43, 44
11	May	45, 46, 47, Sequel

[a]The last part of chapter 8 has been rewritten. In the serial it formed two chapters.
[b]Chapter 11 was revised after serialization.
[c]The last two paragraphs of chapter 32 did not appear in the serial.

The Hand of Ethelberta was published as a volume on 3 April 1876.

The Return of the Native in *Belgravia,* January–December 1878

Part	Date	Chapters in Volume Edition
1	January 1878	Book 1, Chapters 1, 2, 3, 4
2	February	5, 6, 7
3	March	8, 9, 10, 11
4	April	Book 2, Chapters 1, 2, 3, 4, 5
5	May	6, 7, 8
6	June	Book 3, Chapters 1, 2, 3, 4
7	July	5, 6, 7, 8[a]
8	August	Book 4, Chapters 1[b], 2, 3, 4
9	September	5, 6, 7, 8
10	October	Book 5, Chapters 1, 2, 3, 4
11	November	5, 6, 7, 8
12	December	9; Book 6, Chapters 1, 2, 3, 4

[a]Hardy made numerous revisions in book 3, chapter 8 after serialization.
[b]Book 4, chapter 1 was revised considerably for the volume edition.

The Norton Critical Edition (ed. James Gindin) identifies the serial parts.
The Return of the Native was published as a volume on 4 November 1878.

The Trumpet Major in *Good Words,* January–December 1880

Part	Date	Chapters in Volume Edition
1	January 1880	1, 2, 3, 4
2	February	5, 6, 7
3	March	8, 9, 10
4	April	11, 12, 13, 14
5	May	15, 16, 17
6	June	18, 19, 20, 21
7	July	22, 23, 24
8	August	25, 26, 27
9	September	28, 29, 30
10	October	31, 32, 33, 34[a]

The Trumpet Major (cont.)

| 11 | November | 34 (cont.), 35, 36, 37 |
| 12 | December | 38, 39, 40, 41 |

ªOnly the first twenty paragraphs of chapter 34 were included in the serial, the last paragraph commencing "She soon finished her shopping."

The novel was also published serially in the United States in *Demorest's Monthly Magazine* (New York), January 1880–January 1881. *The Trumpet Major* was published as a volume on 26 October 1880.

A Laodicean in **Harper's New Monthly Magazine, December 1880– December 1881**

The volume edition contains minor revisions.

Part	Date	Chapters in Volume Edition
1	December 1880	Book 1, Chapters 1, 2, 3, 4ª
2	January 1881	4 (cont.), 5, 6, 7, 8ᵇ
3	February	8 (cont.), 9, 10, 11, 12
4	March	13, 14, 15; Book 2, Chapters 1, 2ᶜ
5	April	2 (cont.), 3, 4, 5, 6ᵈ
6	May	6 (cont.), 7; Book 3, Chapters 1, 2, 3ᵉ
7	June	3 (cont.), 4, 5, 6, 7
8	July	8, 9, 10, 11
9	August	Book 4, Chapters 1, 2, 3, 4, 5
10	September	Book 5, Chapters 1, 2, 3, 4, 5
11	October	6, 7, 8, 9, 10
12	November	11, 12, 13, 14
13	December	Book 6, Chapters 1, 2, 3, 4, 5

ªPart 1 ends halfway through chapter 4 with "O no. And I never knew one till I knew Paula. I think they are very nice; though I sometimes wish Paula was not one, but the religion of reasonable persons."
ᵇPart 2 ends halfway through chapter 8 with " 'O yes—lots of it!' said Mr. Havill, nettled."

cPart 4 ends halfway through chapter 2 with " 'This is a treatise on the subject,' he said. 'I will teach it to you some day.' "
dPart 5 ends halfway through chapter 6, the last paragraph beginning "As yet it was scarcely dark out of doors."
ePart 6 ends two thirds through the chapter with " 'His wife is dead,' said the messenger."

A *Laodicean* was published as a volume on 25 November 1881 in the United States, during the first week of December in England.

Two on a Tower in *Atlantic Monthly,* May–December 1882

For the volume edition Hardy made numerous minor stylistic revisions.

Part	Date	Chapters in Volume Edition
1	May 1882	1, 2, 3, 4
2	June	5, 6, 7, 8, 9
3	July	10, 11, 12, 13, 14, 15
4	August	16, 17, 18, 19, 20, 21
5	September	22, 23, 24, 25, 26, 27
6	October	28, 29, 30, 31, 32
7	November	33, 34, 35, 36, 37
8	December	38, 39, 40, 41

Two on a Tower was published as a volume at the end of October 1882.

The Mayor of Casterbridge in the *Graphic,* 2 January–15 May 1886

Part	Date	Chapters in Volume Edition
1	2 January 1886	1, 2
2	9 January	3, 4, 5a
3	16 January	5 (cont.), 6, 7
4	23 January	8, 9

The Mayor of Casterbridge (cont.)

5	30 January	10, 11, 12[b]
6	6 February	13, 14, 15[c]
7	13 February	15 (cont.), 16, 17
8	20 February	18[d], 19
9	27 February	20, 21
10	6 March	22, 23
11	13 March	24, 25
12	20 March	26, 27[e]
13	27 March	27 (cont.), 28, 29
14	3 April	30, 31, 32
15	10 April	33, 34[f]
16	17 April	35[g], 36
17	24 April	37, 38
18	1 May	39, 40, 41[h]
19	8 May	41 (cont.), 42, 43[i]
20	15 May	44[j], 45

[a]Part 2 ends halfway through chapter 5 with the paragraph beginning "Oh no; don't ye know him to be the celebrated abstaining worthy of that name?" and ending "yer gospel oath is a serious thing."

[b]Chapter 12 was revised considerably after serialization.

[c]Part 6 ends halfway through chapter 15 with the paragraph beginning "He asked me and he questioned me, and then 'a wouldn't hear my points!"

[d]The first half of chapter 18 was rewritten after serialization.

[e]Part 12 ends two thirds of the way through chapter 27 with the paragraph beginning "Henchard did not hear the reply" and concluding "They went on . . . upon the carts and wagons which carried them away."

[f]The middle part of chapter 34 was revised from the serial.

[g]Thirteen paragraphs in chapter 35 were subsequently omitted from the volume.

[h]Part 18 ends one third of the way through chapter 41 with the paragraph beginning "The sailor continued standing" and concluding "I'll trouble you no longer."

[i]Chapter 43 was revised extensively after serialization.

[j]About half the content of chapter 44 was cut out after serialization.

Richard Little Purdy in *Thomas Hardy: A Bibliographical Study* (London: Oxford Univ. Press, 1954) notes that the revisions in *The Mayor of Casterbridge* "are not, as in the case of several subsequent novels, simply a return to an original unbowdlerized version" (p. 52).

The Norton Critical Edition (ed. James K. Robinson) identifies the serial parts.

The Mayor of Casterbridge was published as a volume on 10 May 1886.

The Woodlanders in *Macmillan's Magazine,* May 1886–April 1887

Part	Date	Chapters in Volume Edition
1	May 1886	1, 2, 3[a], 4
2	June	5, 6, 7, 8
3	July	9, 10, 11, 12, 13
4	August	14, 15, 16, 17, 18
5	September	19, 20[b], 21, 22
6	October	23, 24, 25
7	November	26, 27, 28, 29
8	December	30, 31, 32, 33
9	January 1887	34, 35, 36, 37
10	February	38, 39, 40
11	March	41, 42, 43
12	April	44, 45[c], 46, 47, 48

[a]The middle of chapter 3 was revised slightly for the serial.
[b]Chapter 20 contained some slight bowdlerizations. In particular Hardy left out the final sentence indicating that the two had spent the night in the haycock: "It was daybreak before Fitzpiers and Suke Damson re-entered Little Hintock."
[c]Chapter 45 was revised slightly for the serial.

The Woodlanders was published as a volume on 15 March 1887.

Tess of the D'Urbervilles in the *Graphic,* 4 July–26 December 1891

In order to make this novel suitable for the reading audience of the *Graphic,* Hardy had to make many revisions and omissions, the most significant omissions being chapters 10 and 11 (the seduction of Tess) and chapter 14 (the baptism and death of Tess's baby). The following outline is, therefore, only a rough approximation. For a detailed analysis of revision and omissions see Mary Ellen Chase, *Thomas Hardy from Serial to Novel* (Minneapolis: Univ. of Minnesota Press, 1927), pp. 69–112, and J. T. Laird, *The Shaping of* Tess of the D'Urbervilles (Oxford: Clarendon, 1975).

Part	Date	Chapters in Volume Edition
1	4 July 1891	1, 2, 3[a]
2	18 July	3 (cont.), 4, 5[b]
3	25 July	5 (cont.), 6, 7
4	1 August	8, 9, 12

Tess of the D'Urbervilles (cont.)

5	8 August	13, 15, 16
6	15 August	17, 18
7	22 August	19, 20
8	29 August	21, 22, 23
9	5 September	24, 25[c]
10	12 September	25 (cont.), 26
11	19 September	27, 28
12	26 September	29, 30, 31[d]
13	3 October	31 (cont.), 32, 33[e]
14	10 October	33 (cont.), 34, 35[f]
15	17 October	35 (cont.), 36, 37[g]
16	24 October	37 (cont.), 38, 39
17	31 October	40, 41
18	14 November	42, 43, 44
19	21 November	45, 46
20	28 November	47, 48
21	5 December	49, 50
22	12 December	51, 52
23	19 December	53, 54, 55, 56
24	26 December	57, 58, 59

[a]Part 1 ends two thirds through chapter 3 with the paragraph beginning "The *Compleat Fortune-Teller* was an old thick volume."

[b]Part 2 ends one third through chapter 5 with the paragraph beginning "I thought we were an old family; but this is all new!"

[c]Part 9 ends one third through chapter 25 with "Four months or so of torturing ecstasy in his society—of 'pleasure girdled about with pain.' After that the blackness of unutterable night."

[d]Part 12 ends halfway through chapter 31 with the paragraph beginning "A spiritual forgetfulness co-existed with an intellectual remembrance."

[e]Part 13 ends halfway through chapter 33 with the paragraph beginning "The hurry of dressing and starting left no time for more than this."

[f]Part 14 ends one third through chapter 35 with the paragraph beginning "The image raised caused her to take pity upon herself as one who was ill-used."

[g]Part 15 ends halfway through chapter 37 with the paragraph beginning "Here they were within a plantation which formed the Abbey grounds."

The Norton Critical Edition (ed. Scot Elledge) identifies the serial parts.
Tess of the D'Urbervilles was published as a volume in late November 1891.

The Well-Beloved, published as *The Pursuit of the Well-Beloved* in the *Illustrated London News,* 1 October–17 December 1892

Part	Date	Chapters in Volume Edition
1	1 October 1892	Part 1, Chapters 1[a], 2, 3
2	8 October	4, 5, 6, 7[b]
3	15 October	7 (cont.), 8, 9; Part 2, Chapter 1[c]
4	22 October	1 (cont.), 2, 3
5	29 October	4, 5, 6, 7[d]
6	5 November	7 (cont.), 8, 9
7	12 November	10, 11, 12[e]
8	19 November	12 (cont.), 13; Part 3, Chapter 1[f]
9	26 November	1 (cont.), 2, 3
10	3 December	4, 5[g]
11	10[h] December	
12	17[h] December	

[a]The serial has a chapter that Hardy did not use in the volume (that chapter is not indicated on the outline above). What became chapter 1 in the volume was extensively rewritten from the serial. Chapter 2 of the serial was revised and shortened.

[b]Part 2 of the serial ends with the first sentence of paragraph 9 of chapter 7.

[c]Part 3 of the serial ends halfway through chapter 1 with the paragraph commencing "The lady blushed."

[d]Part 5 ends ten paragraphs into chapter 7 with the paragraph beginning "Engaged in the study of her ear and the nape of her white neck."

[e]Part 7 ends halfway through chapter 12 with "No sooner had the words slipped out than Pierston would have recalled them. He had felt in a moment that they were hazardous."

[f]Part 8 ends three paragraphs short of the chapter end.

[g]Part 10 ends nineteen paragraphs into the chapter.

[h]This portion of the novel was completely rewritten for the volume edition. Hardy changed the plot and substituted a completely new conclusion.

The Well-Beloved was published as a volume on 16 March 1897.

Jude the Obscure in *Harper's New Monthly Magazine,* December 1894–November 1895

Part	Date	Chapters in Volume Edition
1[a]	December 1894	Part First, Chapters 1, 2, 3, 4, 5, 6
2[b]	January 1895	7, 8[c], 9, 10, 11
3	February	Part Second, Chapters 1, 2, 3, 4, 5
4	March	6, 7; Part Third, Chapters 1, 2, 3
5	April	4, 5, 6, 7
6	May	8, 9, 10; Part Fourth, Chapters 1, 2
7	June	3, 4, 5
8	July	6; Part Fifth, Chapters 1, 2, 3
9	August	4, 5, 6, 7
10	September	8; Part Sixth, Chapters 1, 2, 3
11	October	4, 5, 6, 7[d]
12	November	7 (cont.), 8, 9, 10, 11

[a]Part 1 was published under the title *The Simpletons.*

[b]Part 2 was retitled *Hearts Insurgent.* This headnote was attached to the part: "The author's attention having been drawn to the resemblance between the title 'The Simpletons' and that of another English novel [presumably Reade's *A Simpleton* serialized in *London Society* and *Harper's*], he has decided to revert to the title originally selected, viz., 'Hearts Insurgent,' which will therefore be used in future parts of the story."

[c]Beginning with this chapter, Hardy revised the novel to make it acceptable to the magazine audience. The revisions are too extensive to indicate in this outline. For a full discussion of the revisions see Mary Ellen Chase, *Thomas Hardy from Serial to Novel.*

[d]Part 11 concludes eighteen paragraphs short of the end of chapter 7 with the paragraph beginning " 'Don't go,' she said to the guests at parting."

The Norton Critical Edition (ed. Norman Page) identifies the serial parts. *Jude the Obscure* was published as a volume on 1 November 1895.

Charles Kingsley (1819–75)

Yeast, published as *Yeast; or, The Thoughts, Sayings, and Doings of Lancelot Smith, Gentleman* in *Fraser's Magazine,* July–December 1848

Part	Date	Chapters in Volume Edition
1	July 1848	1, 2[a]
2	August	3, 4[b]
3	September	6, 7[c], 9
4	October	10[d], 11
5	November	12, 13
6	December	14, 15[e], 16, 17, Epilogue[f]

[a]The final paragraph was not included in the serial.
[b]Chapter 5 was added for the volume edition.
[c]Chapter 8 was added for the volume edition.
[d]Chapter 10 was expanded for the volume edition.
[e]Chapters 14 and 15 were considerably expanded from one chapter in the serial.
[f]Chapter 17 and the epilogue were revised and expanded for the volume edition.

Hypatia in *Fraser's Magazine,* January 1852–April 1853

Part	Date	Chapters in Volume Edition
1	January 1852	2[a]
2	February	3, 4
3	March	5, 6
4	April	7, 8
5	May	9, 10[b]
6	June	11, 12
7	July	13, 14
8	August	15, 16
9	September	17, 18
10	October	19, 20[c]
11	November	21
12	December	22

Hypatia (cont.)

13	January 1853	23, 24
14	February	25, 26
15	March	27, 28
16	April	29, 30

[a]The preface and chapter 1 were added for the volume edition.
[b]Chapter 10 contains a long section, "The Author to His Readers," that was eventually revised and expanded into the preface to the volume edition.
[c]The final ten paragraphs (following the phrase "Pelagia the wanton") were not included in the serial.

Hereward the Wake, published as *Hereward: The Last of the English*, in *Good Words*, January–December 1860

Part	Date	Chapters in Volume Edition
1	January 1860	Prelude, Chapter 1[a]
2	February	2[b], 3, 4, 5
3	March	6, 7, 8, 9
4	April	10, 11, 12, 13, 14
5	May	15, 16, 17, 18[c]
6	June	19, 20, 21, 22
7	July	23, 24, 25
8	August	26, 27, 28, 29
9	September	30, 31, 32
10	October	33, 34, 35
11	November	36, 37, 38
12[d]	December	39, 40, 41, 42

[a]Chapter 1 was revised for the volume edition.
[b]The "Pedigree of Gospatric and the Dunbars" was not in the serial.
[c]The "Pedigree of the Countess Gyda" was not in the serial.
[d]The chapters of part 12 were revised for the volume edition. The matter of chapter 39 in the volume comprised two chapters in the serial. Much of the narrative of part 12 has been rearranged.

Rudyard Kipling (1865–1936)

The Light That Failed in *Lippincott's Monthly Magazine,* January 1891

The Light That Failed appeared complete in the January 1891 issue of *Lippincott's,* consisting of twelve chapters with the "happy ending." Before the publication in *Lippincott's,* another version with fourteen chapters and the "sad ending" was filed for copyright.

The Naulahka (written in collaboration with Wolcott Balestier) in *Century Magazine,* November 1891–July 1892

Part	Date	Chapters in Volume Edition
1	November 1891	1, 2, 3
2	December	4, 5, 6
3	January 1892	7, 8, 9ᵃ
4	February	9 (cont.), 10, 11
5	March	12, 13
6	April	14, 15, 16, 17
7	May	18, 19
8	June	20
9	July	21

ᵃPart 3 concludes two thirds of the way through chapter 9 with the paragraph beginning "A moment later she recurred to the subject of her mother" and concluding "Why do men go to war?"

The Naulahka was published as a volume in April 1892.

Captains Courageous in *McClure's Magazine,* November 1896–May 1897

Part	Date	Chapters in Volume Edition
1	November 1896	1, 2
2	December	3
3	January 1897	4, 5
4	February	6, 7, 8[a]
5	March	8 (cont.), 9[b]
6	April	9 (cont.), 10[c]
7	May	10 (cont.)

[a]Part 4 ends two thirds of the way through chapter 8, the last paragraph being "Next morning all, except the cook, were rather ashamed of the ceremonies, and went to work double tides, speaking gruffly to one another."

[b]Part 5 ends one third of the way through chapter 9 with the paragraph beginning "To the Western man (though this would not please either city), Chicago and Boston are cheek by jowl."

[c]Part 6 ends one third of the way through chapter 10 with the paragraph "I lost some; and I gained some. I'll tell you."

Captains Courageous in *Pearson's Magazine,* December 1896–April 1897

Part	Date	Chapters in Volume Edition
1	December 1896	1, 2
2	January 1897	3, 4
3	February	5, 6, 7
4	March	8, 9[a]
5	April	9 (cont.), 10

[a]Part 4 ends two thirds of the way through chapter 9. The last paragraph in the part begins "One never knows when one's taking one's biggest risks."

Captains Courageous was published as a volume in October 1897.

Kim in *McClure's Magazine,* December 1900–October 1901

Part	Date	Chapters in Volume Edition
1	December 1900	1
2	January 1901	2, 3[a]
3	February	3 (cont.), 4[b]
4	March	4 (cont.), 5
5	April	6, 7
6	May	8, 9
7	June	10, 11[c]
8	July	11 (cont.), 12[d]
9	August	12 (cont.), 13[e]
10	September	13 (cont.), 14
11	October	15

[a]Part 2 ends halfway through chapter 3 with " 'Be it so—be it so.' The old man nodded his head. 'This is a great and terrible world. I never knew there were so many men alive in it.' "

[b]Part 3 ends two thirds of the way through chapter 4 with the paragraph beginning "He rose and stalked to the cart."

[c]Part 7 ends slightly more than halfway through chapter 11 with "They all piled into it a couple of hours later, and slept through the heat of the day."

[d]Part 8 ends halfway through chapter 12 with "Said the hakim, hardly more than shaping the words with his lips, 'How do you do, Mr. O'Hara? I am jolly glad to see you again.' "

[e]Part 9 ends halfway through chapter 13 with " 'He wishes it now—for money.' "

Kim in *Cassell's Magazine*, January–November 1901

Part	Date	Chapters in Volume Edition
1	January 1901	1
2	February	2, 3
3	March	4
4	April	5, 6[a]
5	May	6 (cont.), 7
6	June	8, 9[b]
7	July	9 (cont.), 10
8	August	11, 12[c]
9	September	12 (cont.), 13[d]
10	October	13 (cont.), 14
11	November	15

[a]Part 4 concludes halfway through chapter 6 with "They'll teach ye something—but I don't think ye'll like it."

[b]Part 6 ends halfway through chapter 9, the last paragraph beginning "And I will see that thou art well taught."

[c]Part 8 ends one third of the way through chapter 12, the last paragraph beginning "And he told stories, tracing with a finger in the dust."

[d]Part 9 ends halfway through chapter 13 with the sentence "He thanked all the Gods of Hindustan, and Herbert Spencer, that there remained some valuables to steal."

Kim was published as a volume in October 1901.

Edward Lytton Bulwer-Lytton, First Baron Lytton (1803–73)

The Caxtons in *Blackwood's Magazine,* **April 1848–October 1849**

Part	Date	Chapters in Volume Edition
1	April 1848	Part 1, Chapters 1, 2, 3, 4, 5, 6
2	May	Part 2, Chapters 1, 2, 3, 4, 5
3	June	Part 3, Chapters 1, 2, 3, 4, 5, 6, 7, 8
4	July	Part 4, Chapters 1, 2, 3, 4, 5, 6
5	August	Part 5, Chapters 1, 2, 3, 4
6	September	Part 6, Chapters 1, 2, 3, 4, 5, 6, 7, 8
7	October	Part 7, Chapters 1, 2, 3, 4, 5, 6, 7, 8, 9
8	December[a]	Part 8, Chapters 1, 2, 3, 4
9	January 1849	Part 9, Chapters 1, 2, 3, 4, 5, 6, 7
10	February	Part 10, Chapters 1, 2, 3, 4, 5, 6
11	March	Part 11, Chapters 1, 2, 3, 4, 5, 6, 7
12	April	Part 12, Chapters 1, 2, 3, 4, 5, 6, 7
13	June[b]	Part 13, Chapters 1, 2, 3, 4, 5, 6; Part 14, Chapters 1, 2, 3, 4, 5, 6, 7, 8
14	July	Part 15, Chapters 1, 2, 3, 4
15	August	Part 16, Chapters 1, 2, 3, 4, 5, 6, 7, 8, 9, 10, 11
16	September	Part 17, Chapters 1, 2, 3, 4, 5, 6
17	October	Part 18, Chapters 1, 2, 3, 4, 5, 6, 7, 8

[a]There was no installment for November.
[b]No installment appeared for May. All of the material in the June installment was published as part 13; it was divided into two parts for the book edition.

My Novel; or, Varieties in English Life "by Pisistratus Caxton" in Blackwood's Magazine, September 1850–January 1853

Part	Date	Chapters in Volume Edition
1	September 1850	Book 1, Chapters 1, 2, 3, 4, 5, 6, 7, 8, 9
2	October	10, 11, 12, 13
3	November	Book 2, Chapters 1, 2, 3, 4, 5, 6
4	December	7, 8, 9, 10, 11, 12
5	January 1851	Book 3, Chapters 1, 2, 3, 4, 5, 6, 7, 8, 9, 10, 11, 12
6	February	13, 14, 15, 16, 17, 18, 19, 20, 21, 22, 23, 24, 25, 26, 27, 28, 29
7	March	Book 4, Chapters 1, 2, 3, 4, 5, 6, 7, 8, 9, 10, 11, 12
8	April	13, 14, 15, 16, 17, 18, 19, 20, 21, 22, 23, 24, 25
9	May	Book 5, Chapters 1, 2, 3, 4, 5, 6
10	June	7, 8, 9, 10, 11, 12, 13, 14, 15, 16, 17, 18, 19
11	July	Book 6, Chapters 1, 2, 3, 4, 5, 6, 7, 8, 9, 10, 11, 12
12	August	13, 14, 15, 16, 17, 18, 19, 20, 21, 22, 23, 24, 25[a]
13	September	Book 7, Chapters 1, 2, 3, 4, 5, 6, 7, 8, 9, 10, 11, 12, 13, 14, 15
14	October	16, 17, 18, 19, 20, 21, 22
15	November	Book 8, Chapters 1, 2, 3, 4, 5, 6
16	December	7, 8, 9, 10, 11, 12, 13, 14
17	January 1852	Book 9, Chapters 1, 2, 3, 4, 5, 6, 7, 8
18	February	9, 10, 11, 12, 13, 14, 15, 16, 17
19	March	Book 10, Chapters 1, 2, 3, 4, 5, 6, 7, 8, 9
20	April	10, 11, 12, 13, 14, 15, 16, 17, 18, 19, 20, 21, 22, 23, 24, 25
21	May	Book 11, Chapters 1, 2, 3, 4, 5, 6, 7, 8, 9, 10, 11, 12
22	July[b]	13, 14, 15, 16
23	August	17, 18, 19, 20
24	September	Book 12, Chapters 1, 2, 3, 4, 5, 6, 7, 8
25	October	9, 10, 11, 12, 13, 14, 15, 16, 17, 18
26	November	19, 20, 21, 22, 23
27	December	24, 25, 26, 27, 28, 29, 30
28	January 1853	31, 32, 33, 34, Final Chapter

[a]The "Note on Homeopathy" was not included in the serial.
[b]There was no installment for June.

What Will He Do with It? "by Pisistratus Caxton" in *Blackwood's Magazine*, June 1857–January 1859

Part	Date	Chapters in Volume Edition
1	June 1857	Book 1, Chapters 1, 2, 3, 4, 5, 6, 7, 8
2	July	9, 10, 11, 12, 13, 14, 15, 16, 17, 18, 19
3	August	Book 2, Chapters 1, 2, 3, 4, 5, 6, 7, 8, 9, 10, 11, 12
4	September	13, 14, 15; Book 3, Chapters 1, 2, 3, 4, 5, 6, 7, 8
5	October	9, 10, 11, 12
6	November	13, 14, 15, 16, 17, 18, 19, 20, 21
7	December	22, 23, 24; Book 4, Chapters 1, 2, 3, 4
8	January 1858	5, 6, 7, 8, 9, 10, 11, 12, 13, 14
9	February	15, 16, 17, 18, 19; Book 5, Chapters 1, 2, 3, 4
10	March	5, 6, 7, 8, 9, 10
11	April	Book 6[a], Chapters 1, 2, 3, 4, 5
12	May	6, 7, 8, 9; Book 7, Chapters 1, 2, 3, 4
13	June	5, 6, 7
14	July	8, 9, 10, 11, 12, 13, 14, 15, 16
15	August	17, 18, 19, 20, 21, 22, 23, 24, 25; Book 8, Chapters 1, 2, 3
16	September	4, 5, 6, 7, 8, 9; Book 9, Chapter 1
17	October	2, 3; Book 10, Chapters 1, 2, 3
18	November	4, 5, 6, 7, 8; Book 11, Chapters 1, 2, 3
19	December	4, 5, 6, 7, 8, 9, 10, 11; Book 12, Chapters 1, 2, 3
20	January 1859	4, 5, 6, 7, 8, 9, 10, 11, 12

[a]Part 11 contains an additional chapter, not included in the volume, that answers critics of the serial.

A Strange Story in *All the Year Round,* 10 August 1861–8 March 1862

Part	Date	Chapters in Volume Edition
1	10 August 1861	1, 2
2	17 August	3, 4, 5, 6
3	24 August	7, 8
4	31 August	9, 10, 11, 12
5	7 September	13, 14, 15
6	14 September	16, 17
7	21 September	18, 19, 20, 21
8	28 September	22, 23
9	5 October	24
10	12 October	25, 26, 27
11	19 October	28, 29
12	26 October	30, 31
13	2 November	32, 33
14	9 November	34, 35
15	16 November	36, 37, 38
16	23 November	39
17	30 November	40
18	7 December	41, 42
19	14 December	43, 44, 45
20	21 December	46, 47, 48, 49, 50
21	28 December	51, 52, 53, 54
22	4 January 1862	55, 56
23	11 January	57, 58, 59, 60, 61
24	18 January	62, 63, 64, 65, 66, 67
25	25 January	68, 69, 70, 71
26	1 February	72, 73
27	8 February	74
28	15 February	75, 76
29	22 February	77, 78, 79, 80
30	1 March	81, 82, 83, 84, 85, 86
31	8 March	87, 88, 89

The Parisians "by E—— G——" in *Blackwood's Magazine,* October 1872–January 1874

Part	Date	Chapters in Volume Edition
1	October 1872	Introductory Chapter; Book 1, Chapters 1, 2, 3, 4, 5, 6, 7, 8
2	November	Book 2, Chapters 1, 2, 3, 4, 5, 6, 7, 8
3	December	Book 3, Chapters 1, 2, 3, 4, 5, 6, 7, 8, 9, 10
4	January 1873	Book 4, Chapters 1, 2, 3, 4, 5, 6, 7, 8, 9
5	February	Book 5, Chapters 1, 2, 3
6	March	4, 5, 6, 7, 8, 9, 10, 11
7	April	Book 6, Chapters 1, 2, 3, 4, 5
8	May	6, 7, 8
9	June	Book 7, Chapters 1, 2, 3, 4, 5, 6
10	July	Book 8, Chapters 1, 2, 3, 4, 5
11	August	Book 9, Chapters 1, 2, 3, 4, 5, 6, 7, 8, 9, 10, 11, 12, 13, 14, 15
12	September	Book 10, Chapters 1, 2, 3, 4, 5, 6, 7
13	October	Book 11, Chapters 1, 2, 3, 4, 5, 6, 7
14	November	8, 9, 10, 11, 12, 13, 14, 15, 16, 17, 18
15	December	Book 12, Chapters 1, 2, 3, 4
16[a]	January 1874	5, 6, 7, 8, 9, 10, 11, 12, 13, 14[b]

[a]The part contains two notes by the author's son, Robert Bulwer-Lytton, one at the beginning and one at the end of the part.
[b]The novel is incomplete.

Frederick Marryat (1792–1848)

Peter Simple in Metropolitan Magazine, June 1832–September 1833

Part	Date	Chapters in Volume Edition
1	June 1832	1, 2, 3
2	July	4, 5, 6, 7
3	August	8, 9
4	September	10, 11, 12[a]
5	October	12 (cont.), 13
6	November	14, 15[b]
7	December	15 (cont.), 16[c]
8	January 1833	16 (cont.)
9	February	17
10	March	18, 19, 20, 21
11	April	22, 23, 24
12	May	25, 26, 27, 28
13	June	29, 30, 31
14	July	32, 33
15	August	34, 35, 36, 37, 38[d]
16	September	38 (cont.), 39, 40, 41, 42[e]

[a]Part 4 ends six paragraphs into chapter 12 with the paragraph commencing " 'Oh, you are!' replied Mr. Chucks" and concluding "I am obliged too often to sacrifice my gentility."
[b]Only the first paragraph of chapter 15 is included in part 6.
[c]Only the first seven paragraphs of chapter 16 are included; part 7 concludes with "what a precious twisting we should get tomorrow at six bells!"
[d]Part 15 ends one fifth of the way through chapter 38, the last paragraph commencing "This was not very likely to take place."
[e]The remaining twenty-three chapters were not published in the serial. In an essay at the conclusion of the last installment Marryat says that his object in discontinuing the serial is to encourage the readers to buy the book.

Peter Simple was published as a volume in December 1833.

Jacob Faithful in Metropolitan Magazine, September 1833–October 1834

Part	Date	Chapters in Volume Edition
1	September 1833	1
2	October	2, 3[a]
3	November	3 (cont.), 4, 5
4	December	6, 7
5	January 1834	8, 9, 10[b]
6[c]	February	10 (cont.), 11, 12, 13
7	March	14, 15, 16, 17, 18
8	April	19, 20, 21
9	May	22, 23, 24, 25
10	June	26, 27, 28
11	July	29, 30, 31, 32, 33, 34, 35, 36
12	August	37, 38, 39
13	September	40, 41, 42, 43[d]
14	October	43 (cont.), 44, 45, 46

[a]Part 2 ends halfway through chapter 3 with the paragraph beginning "Not having at hand the simile synthetical, we have resorted to the antithetical."
[b]Part 5 ends almost halfway through chapter 10 with the paragraph beginning "The judge then passed the sentence of death upon Marables" and ending "Marables was sentenced to fourteen years' transportation, which, however, before his sailing was commuted to seven."
[c]Part 6 has this note: "In reply to several letters requesting to know if 'Jacob Faithful' will be finished in the 'Metropolitan,' we state, that such is our intention."
[d]Part 13 ends with the first two paragraphs of chapter 43.

Because the novel was not divided into chapters for the serial, most of the lines of verse heading the chapters in the volume were not included.
Jacob Faithful was published as a volume in November or December 1834.

Japhet in Search of a Father in Metropolitan Magazine, November 1834–January 1836

Part	Date	Chapters in Volume Edition
1	November 1834	1, 2, 3, 4, 5, 6[a]
2	December	6 (cont.)[b], 7, 8, 9, 10, 11, 12, 13

Japhet in Search of a Father (cont.)

3	January 1835	14, 15, 16, 17, 18, 19, 20
4	February	21, 22, 23, 24, 25
5	March	26, 27, 28, 29, 30, 31, 32ᶜ
6	April	32 (cont.), 33, 34, 35, 36, 37, 38, 39, 40, 41ᵈ
7	May	41 (cont.), 42, 43, 44, 45, 46, 47, 48, 49ᵉ
8	June	49 (cont.), 50, 51, 52, 53
9	July	54, 55, 56
10	August	57, 58, 59, 60
11	September	61, 62, 63, 64
12	October	65, 66, 67, 68, 69, 70, 71, 72ᶠ
13	November	72 (cont.), 73, 74, 75
14	December	76, 77
15	January 1836	78, 79

ªThe material at the end of part 1 was subsequently reduced to what is now the first three paragraphs of chapter 6.

ᵇPart 2 commences with the fourth paragraph of chapter 6.

ᶜPart 5 ends eight paragraphs short of the end of chapter 32, the last paragraph commencing "Farewell, Newland" and concluding "His lordship shook hands with me, and I took my leave."

ᵈPart 6 ends nine paragraphs into chapter 41 with "This advice I certainly could not consent to follow."

ᵉPart 7 ends with the second paragraph of chapter 49.

ᶠPart 12 ends with the first paragraph of chapter 72.

Japhet in Search of a Father was published as a volume in early January 1836.

Mr. Midshipman Easy in *Metropolitan Magazine*, August 1836

The first four chapters of this novel appeared in the magazine with the following headnote: "We have it in our power to favour our readers with a specimen of the forthcoming new novel, by Captain Marryat, which holds out the promise of excelling all his hitherto excellent naval novels." The complete novel was published in September 1836.

Snarleyyow; or, The Dog Fiend in *Metropolitan Magazine,* January 1836–June 1837

Part	Date	Chapters in Volume Edition
1	January 1836	1, 2, 3
2	February	4, 5
3	March	6, 7, 8
4	April	9
5	May	10, 11, 12
6	June	13, 14, 15, 16, 17
7	July	18, 19, 20
8	August	21
9	September	22
10	October	23
11	November	24
12	December	25, 26
13	January 1837	27, 28
14	February	29
15	March	30, 31, 32
16	April	33, 34, 35, 36
17	May	37, 38
18	June	39[a]

[a]The final sixteen chapters of the novel (40–55) were not serialized.

Snarleyyow was published as a volume in June 1837.

The Phantom Ship in the *New Monthly Magazine,* March 1837– August 1839

Part	Date	Chapters in Volume Edition
1	March 1837	1, 2
2	April	3, 4, 5
3	May	6, 7, 8
4	June	9
5	July	10, 11
6	August	12

The Phantom Ship (cont.)

7	September	13, 14
8	October	15
9	January 1838[a]	16
10	February	17, 18
11	February 1839[b]	19, 20, 21
12	March	22, 23, 24, 25, 26
13	April	27, 28, 29, 30, 31
14	May	32, 33, 34, 35
15	June	36, 37, 38
16	July	39
17	August	40, 41, 42

[a]No installments appeared in the November and December 1837 issues.
[b]The serial was interrupted by Marryat's trip to America.

The Phantom Ship was published as a volume in April 1839.

Poor Jack in twelve monthly parts, January–December 1840

Part	Date	Chapters in Volume Edition
1	January 1840	1, 2, 3, 4, 5, 6[a]
2	February	6 (cont.), 7, 8, 9, 10
3	March	11, 12, 13
4	April	14, 15, 16, 17, 18
5	May	19, 20, 21, 22
6	June	23, 24, 25, 26, 27
7	July	28, 29, 30, 31
8	August	32, 33, 34, 35
9	September	36, 37, 38, 39
10	October	40, 41, 42, 43, 44
11	November	45, 46, 47, 48
12	December	49, 50, 51, Finale

[a]Part 1 concludes halfway through chapter 6 in the middle of a sentence: "No, my man, you must not fish without permission; and."

Poor Jack was published as a volume on 1 December 1840.

Joseph Rushmore, **published as** *The Poacher* **in the** *Era,* **13 December 1840–23 May 1841**

Part	Date	Chapters in Volume Edition
1	13 December 1840	1, 2, 3, 4
2	20 December	5, 6, 7
3	27 December	8, 9, 10
4	3 January 1841	11, 12, 13
5	10 January	14, 15
6	17 January	16, 17, 18
7	24 January	19, 20, 21
8	31 January	22
9	7 February	23, 24
10	14 February	25, 26
11	21 February	27
12	28 February	28
13	7 March	29, 30, 31
14	14 March	32, 33
15	21 March	34
16	28 March	35, 36
17	4 April	37, 38
18	11 April	39, 40
19	18 April	41, 42
20	25 April	43
21	2 May	44
22	9 May	45
23	16 May	46, 47, 48
24	23 May	49, 50

Joseph Rushmore was published as a volume in June 1841.

The Privateer's Man in the New Monthly Magazine, August 1845– June 1846

Part	Date	Chapters in Volume Edition
1	August 1845	1[a]
2	September	2, 3
3	October	4, 5
4	November	6, 7
5	December	8, 9
6	January 1846	10, 11
7	February	12, 13[b]
8	March	14, 15
9	April	16
10	May	17[c]
11	June	17 (cont.)

[a]The editor, W. Harrison Ainsworth, wrote to Marryat after the publication of part 1: "You must give us a longer 'extract,' twelve pages or a sheet, next month"; hence, the subsequent parts are all more lengthy.
[b]In the serial the chapters begin renumbering after chapter 12.
[c]Part 10 ends halfway through chapter 17 with the paragraph beginning "I was demurring."

The Privateer's Man was published as a volume in July 1846.

Children of the New Forest

Children of the New Forest was planned for part issue. Part 1 was published April 1847. Michael Sadleir (Nineteenth Century Fiction [Berkeley: Univ. of California Press, 1951], I, 230) states that part 1 comprised pages one through seventy-two of the first edition and notes that he is "practically certain" that no parts beyond the first one were ever issued. Volume 1 was published in July 1847, volume 2 in October.

George Meredith (1828–1909)

Evan Harrington in *Once a Week*, 11 February–13 October 1860

Part	Date	Chapters in Volume Edition
1	11 February 1860	1, 2, 3
2	18 February	4
3	25 February	5, 6
4	3 March	7
5	10 March	8
6	17 March	9
7	24 March	10
8	31 March	11, 12
9	7 April	13
10	14 April	14
11	21 April	15
12	28 April	16
13	5 May	17
14	12 May	18
15	19 May	19, 20
16	26 May	21, 22
17	2 June	23
18	9 June	24
19	16 June	25
20	23 June	26
21	30 June	27
22	7 July	28
23	14 July	29
24	21 July	30
25	28 July	31
26	4 August	32
27	11 August	33
28	18 August	34, 35
29	25 August	36, 37
30	1 September	38, 39
31	8 September	40
32	15 September	41

Evan Harrington (cont.)

33	22 September	42, 43
34	29 September	44
35	6 October	45
36	13 October	46

The novel was revised slightly after serialization, but the text is essentially the same. Often the text of the volume has been shortened by the removal of paragraphs from the serial.

Vittoria in the *Fortnightly Review,* 15 January–1 December 1866

Part	Date	Chapters in Volume Edition
1	15 January 1866	1, 2, 3
2	1 February	4, 5, 6, 7
3	15 February	8, 9
4	1 March	10, 11
5	15 March	12, 13
6	1 April	14, 15
7	15 April	16, 17, 18
8	1 May	19, 20
9	15 May	21, 22
10	1 June	23, 24
11	15 June	25, 26
12	1 July	27
13	15 July	28, 29
14	1 August	30, 31
15	15 August	32
16	1 September	33, 34
17	15 September	35, 36
18	1 October	37, 38
19	15 October	39, 40
20	1 November	41, 42, 43, 44
21	1 December	45, 46, Epilogue

Vittoria was published as a volume on 20 December 1866.

The Adventures of Harry Richmond in the *Cornhill Magazine*, September 1870–November 1871

Part	Date	Chapters in Volume Edition
1	September 1870	1, 2, 3, 4
2	October	5, 6, 7
3	November	8, 9, 10, 11, 12
4	December	13, 14, 15, 16
5	January 1871	17, 18, 19, 20, 21
6	February	22, 23, 24, 25, 26
7	March	27, 28, 29, 30, 31, 32[a]
8	April	33, 34, 35
9	May	36, 37, 38
10	June	39, 40, 41
11	July	42, 43, 44[b]
12	August	44 (cont.), 45, 46, 47
13	September	48, 49, 50
14	October	51, 52, 53
15[c]	November	54, 55, 56

[a]Ten sentences at the end of part 7 of the serial were dropped from the volume edition.

[b]Chapter 44 was composed of two chapters in the serial so that one portion was in part 11, the remainder in part 12. For the volume the material was rearranged and rewritten extensively.

[c]The material of part 15 was reduced by almost half for the volume edition.

The University of Nebraska Press edition (ed. L. T. Hergenhan, 1970) contains an appendix, "Alterations to the Serial Text, and the 'Second Edition.' "

The Adventures of Harry Richmond was published as a volume on 26 October 1871.

Beauchamp's Career in the *Fortnightly Review*, August 1874– December 1875

Part	Date	Chapters in Volume Edition
1	August 1874	1, 2, 3
2	September	4, 5, 6, 7, 8
3	October	9, 10, 11
4	November	12, 13, 14

Beauchamp's Career (cont.)

5	December	15, 16, 17
6	January 1875	18, 19
7	February	20, 21, 22
8	March	23, 24, 25
9	April	26, 27, 28
10	May	29, 30, 31
11	June	32, 33, 34
12	July	35, 36, 37
13	August	38, 39, 40
14	September	41, 42, 43
15	October	44, 45, 46
16	November	47, 48, 49, 50, 51
17	December	52, 53, 54, 55, 56

Beauchamp's Career was published as a volume in November 1875.

The Egoist, published as *Sir Willoughby Patterne the Egoist* in the *Glasgow Weekly Herald*, 21 June 1879–10 January 1880

Part	Date	Chapters in Volume Edition
1	21 June 1879	Prelude, 1, 2, 3
2	28 June	4, 5
3	5 July	6, 7
4	12 July	8, 9
5	19 July	10
6	26 July	11, 12
7	2 August	13, 14
8	9 August	15, 16
9	16 August	17, 18
10	23 August	19
11	30 August	20, 21[a]
12	6 September	21 (cont.), 22
13	13 September	23
14	20 September	24, 25[b]

The Egoist (cont.)

15	27 September	25 (cont.), 26
16	4 October	27, 28
17	11 October	29
18	18 October	30, 31
19	25 October	32, 33
20	1 November	34
21	8 November	35
22	15 November	36, 37
23	22 November	38, 39
24	29 November	40, 41ᶜ
25	6 December	41 (cont.), 42ᵈ
26	13 December	43, 44ᵉ
27	20 December	44 (cont.), 45
28	27 December	46, 47ᶠ
29	3 January 1880	47 (cont.), 48
30	10 January	49, 50

ᵃPart 11 contains only the first twenty-nine paragraphs of the chapter; the last paragraph in the part begins, "She blotted it out, kept it from her mind."

ᵇOnly about one third of chapter 25 is included; the part ends with "The more you like him, the more I shall like you, Crossjay."

ᶜPart 24 ends halfway through chapter 41 with "Willoughby wheeled and waylaid him with a bound."

ᵈThe last paragraph of the chapter is missing from the serial.

ᵉPart 26 ends almost halfway through chapter 44 with " 'In all her relations, Mr. Dale!' 'It is my prayer,' he said."

ᶠPart 28 ends one third of the way through chapter 47 with: " 'My wish is to please you.' 'You could?' 'I said so.' "

The Egoist was published as a volume in October 1879.

The Tragic Comedians in the *Fortnightly Review*, October 1880– February 1881

Part	Date	Chapters in Volume Edition
1	October 1880	1, 2ᵃ, 3, 4ᵃ
2	November	5, 6, 7

The Tragic Comedians (cont.)

3	December	8, 9, 10
4	January 1881	11, 12, 13, 14
5	February	15, 16, 17, 18, 19

ªChapters 2 and 4 were revised slightly for the volume edition.

The Tragic Comedians was published as a volume on 15 December 1880.

Diana of the Crossways in the *Fortnightly Review*, June–December 1884

Part	Date	Chapters in Volume Edition
1	June 1884	1, 2, 3
2	July	4, 5, 6, 7
3	September	8, 9, 10, 11, 12
4	October	13, 14, 15, 16ª
5	November	18, 20, 25
6	December	26, 29ᵇ, 30, 31, 32, 33, 34, 36ᶜ

Many of the chapters are considerably expanded in the volume edition. Note that nine chapters were added after serial publication.

ªPart 4 ends nine paragraphs before the end of chapter 16 with the sentence "It was then settled for Diana to rejoin them the next evening at Lugano, thence to proceed to Luino on the Maggiore."

ᵇOnly the last twenty-four paragraphs of chapter 29 were included in part 6.

ᶜThe serial concludes at the end of chapter 36 with this note: "Thus was the erratic woman stricken; and those who care for more of Diana of the Crossways will find it in the extended chronicle." The "extended chronicle" goes on in the volume edition for seven more chapters in addition to the chapters and passages inserted after serialization.

Diana of the Crossways was published as a volume on 16 February 1885.

One of Our Conquerors in the *Fortnightly Review*, October 1890–May 1891

Meredith so thoroughly rewrote the novel before it appeared as a volume, revising, expanding, and moving chapters about, that a simple outline cannot correlate the serial to the book. The volume was published 15 April 1891.

The Amazing Marriage in *Scribner's Magazine*, January–December 1895

Part	Date	Chapters in Volume Edition
1	January 1895	1, 2, 3, 4
2	February	5, 6, 7, 8
3	March	9, 10, 11, 12
4	April	13, 14, 15, 16
5	May	17, 18, 19, 20
6	June	21, 22, 23, 24
7	July	25, 26, 27, 28
8	August	29, 30, 31
9	September	32, 33, 34, 35, 36
10	October	37, 38[a], 39, 40
11	November	41, 42, 43, 44, 45
12	December	46, 47

[a]Chapters 38 and 39 were rewritten extensively for the serial. Meredith had written to his publisher, "My son has telegraphed that your office is at liberty to reduce for serial purposes the length of my novel. I am sure you have in your staff one to whom I can confide as I would to Mr. Bridges this surgical operation which shall lop excesses without wounding an artery. This without damage to the full publication subsequently, for if I have been criminal in running to this excess, it has come of my conscience in regard to thoroughness" (*The Letters of George Meredith*, ed. C. L. Cline [Oxford: Oxford Univ. Press, 1970], III, 1176).

The Amazing Marriage was published as a volume on 15 November 1895.

Celt and Saxon in the *Fortnightly Review*, January–August 1910

Part	Date	Chapters in Volume Edition
1	January 1910	1, 2, 3
2	February	4, 5, 6
3	March	7, 8
4	April	9, 10, 11
5	May	12, 13
6	June	14, 15
7	July	16, 17
8	August	18, 19[a]

[a]Part 8 ends with a footnote from the editor: "Mr. George Meredith's MS. ends here, the novel remaining unfinished.—ed. F. R." Meredith had died 18 May 1909.

Celt and Saxon was published as a volume in July 1910.

Charles Reade (1814–84)

Double Marriage; or, White Lies, **published as** *White Lies* **in the** *London Journal,* **11 July–5 December 1857.**

After serialization, the novel was revised so extensively that it is impossible to correlate chapters in the serial and the volume. The volume was published in December 1857.

The Cloister and the Hearth, **published as** *A Good Fight* **in** *Once a Week,* **2 July–1 October 1859**

Part	Date	Chapters in Volume Edition
1	2 July 1859	1
2	9 July	2
3	16 July	3
4	23 July	4, 5, 6
5	30 July	7, 8[a]
6	6 August	8 (cont.), 9[b]
7	13 August	9 (cont.), 10[c]
8	20 August	10 (cont.), 11, 12, 13
9	27 August	14, 15, 16, 17
10	3 September	18, 19, 20[d]
11	10 September	20 (cont.), 21, 22, 23[e]
12	17 September	
13	24 September	
14	1 October	

[a]Part 5 stops eleven paragraphs short of the end of chapter 8 with the sentence "It was the leopard."
[b]Part 6 ends nine paragraphs before the end of chapter 9 with "And with this wild, bitter speech, he flung away home and left Margaret weeping."

ᶜPart 7 concludes seven paragraphs short of the end of chapter 10 with "they had never seen a human being killed."

ᵈPart 10 ends eleven paragraphs short of the end of chapter 20 with "After the first impulse she peered through her fingers, her heart panting at her throat."

ᵉChapter 23 was extensively rewritten for the volume edition. Beyond chapter 23 the outline of serial parts is meaningless, for Reade, finding that he could not deal with the editor of the magazine, gave the novel a hurried happy ending.

The revised novel was published as a volume in October 1861.

Hard Cash, published as Very Hard Cash in All the Year Round, 28 March–26 December 1863

Part	Date	Chapters in Volume Edition
1	28 March 1863	Prologue, Chapter 1ᵃ
2	4 April	1 (cont.)
3	11 April	2
4	18 April	3ᵇ
5	25 April	3 (cont.)ᶜ
6	2 May	3 (cont.)
7	9 May	4ᵈ
8	16 May	4 (cont.)
9	23 May	5
10	30 May	6
11	6 June	7, 8
12	13 June	11ᵉ, 9
13	20 June	10
14	27 June	12
15	4 July	13
16	11 July	14, 15
17	18 July	16, 17, 18, 19
18	25 July	20
19	1 August	21, 22, 23
20	8 August	24
21	15 August	25
22	22 August	26, 27

Hard Cash (cont.)

23	29 August	28
24	5 September	29, 34ᵉ
25	12 September	35, 36
26	19 September	30
27	26 September	31
28	3 October	32
29	10 October	33, 37
30	17 October	38
31	24 October	39
32	31 October	40
33	7 November	41, 42
34	14 November	43
35	21 November	44
36	28 November	45
37	5 December	46, 47, 48
38	12 December	49, 50
39	19 December	51, 52, 53ᶠ
40	26 December	53 (cont.), 54

ᵃPart 1 ends one third through chapter 1 with "The race was over. But who had won our party could not see, and must wait to learn."

ᵇPart 4 ends one third through chapter 3 with " 'Well, I will,' said he carelessly; and all his fire died out of him. 'Put out your tongue!—Now your pulse.' "

ᶜPart 5 ends two thirds through chapter 3 with "Sarah, the black-eyed housemaid answered the door.' "

ᵈPart 7 ends halfway through chapter 4 with the paragraph beginning "The two ladies eyed one another silent, yet expressive."

ᵉNote the rearrangement of chapters.

ᶠPart 39 ends one third through chapter 53 with "A solemn, passionless voice seemed to fall on them from the clouds: 'No; it is Mine.' "

Hard Cash was published as a volume on 15 December 1863.

Griffith Gaunt in *Argosy,* December 1865–November 1866

Part	Date	Chapters in Volume Edition
1	December 1865	1, 2, 3, 4[a]
2	January 1866	4 (cont.), 5
3	February	6, 7, 8
4	March	9, 10, 11, 12, 13, 14
5	April	15, 16, 17
6	May	18, 19, 20, 21, 22, 23, 24, 25
7	June	26, 27
8	July	28, 29, 30, 31, 32[b]
9	August	33, 34, 35, 36, 37, 38
10	September	39, 40, 41
11	October	42
12	November	43, 44, 45, 46

[a]Part 1 includes only thirteen paragraphs of chapter 4, ending with "fixed her great grey eyes full and searching on Griffith Gaunt."
[b]Chapters 31 and 32 were one chapter in the serial.

Griffith Gaunt was published as a volume in October 1866.

Foul Play in *Once a Week,* 4 January–20 June 1868

Part	Date	Chapters in Volume Edition
1	4 January 1868	1, 2, 3
2	11 January	4, 5, 6
3	18 January	7, 8
4	25 January	9, 10
5	1 February	11, 12, 13
6	8 February	14, 15[a]
7	15 February	15 (cont.), 16, 17, 18
8	22 February	19, 20, 21, 22
9	29 February	23
10	7 March	24
11	14 March	25, 26
12	21 March	27, 28, 29, 30, 31

Foul Play (cont.)

13	28 March	32, 33, 34
14	4 April	35
15	11 April	36, 37, 38, 39
16	18 April	40, 41, 42, 43
17	25 April	44, 45, 46, 47
18	2 May	48, 49
19	9 May	50, 51
20	16 May	52, 53, 54
21	23 May	55, 56, 57, 58
22	30 May	59, 60, 61
23	6 June	62
24	13 June	63, 64, 65
25	20 June	66

ᵃPart 6 concludes eight paragraphs short of the end of chapter 15 with " 'What ship did she sail in?' said Arthur. 'In one of your own ships—the Proserpine.' "

Foul Play was published as a volume in November or December 1868.

Put Yourself in His Place in the *Cornhill Magazine,* March 1869–July 1870

Part	Date	Chapters in Volume Edition
1	March 1869	1, 2, 3
2	April	4, 5
3	May	6, 7
4	June	8, 9
5	July	10
6	August	11
7	September	12
8	October	13, 14, 15, 16, 17, 18, 19
9	November	20, 21, 22
10	December	23, 24, 25, 26, 27
11	January 1870	28, 29
12	February	30, 31, 32

Put Yourself in His Place (cont.)

13	March	33, 34, 35, 36, 37
14	April	38, 39
15	May	40, 41
16	June	42, 43, 44
17	July	45, 46, 47, 48

Put Yourself in His Place was published as a volume in June 1870.

A Terrible Temptation in *Cassell's Magazine*, April–September 1871

Cassell's Magazine was published weekly between 2 May 1868 and 7 November 1874. Because the only run I was able to examine, the one at the British Library, is bound in monthly, not weekly, covers, I am able to indicate the content by months only.

Part	Date	Chapters in Volume Edition
1	April 1871	1, 2, 3, 4, 5, 6, 7
2	May	8, 9, 10, 11, 12
3	June	13, 14, 15, 16, 17, 18, 19, 20
4	July	21, 22, 23, 24, 25, 26, 27, 28
5	August	29, 30, 31, 32, 33, 34, 35, 36
6	September	37, 38, 39, 40, 41, 42, 43, 44

The note appended to the volume did not appear in the serial.

A Terrible Temptation was published as a volume in August 1871. M. L. Parrish in *Wilkie Collins and Charles Reade* (London: Constable, 1940) says, "It was also published in Four Parts in 1871, by James R. Osgood and Company, Parts I and II being a double number" (p. 233).

A Simpleton in *London Society,* August 1872–September 1873

Part	Date	Chapters in Volume Edition
1	August 1872	1, 2
2	September	3
3	October	4
4	November	5, 6
5	December	7
6	January 1873	8, 9
7	February	10, 11, 12
8	March	13
9	April	14
10	May	15, 16, 17, 18
11	June	19, 20, 21, 22
12	July	23, 24
13	August	25, 26
14	September	27, 28

A Simpleton was published as a volume on 8 August 1873.

A Woman Hater in *Blackwood's Magazine,* June 1876–June 1877

Part	Date	Chapters in Volume Edition
1	June 1876	1, 2
2	July	3, 4, 5[a]
3	August	5 (cont.), 6, 7
4	September	8, 9, 10[b]
5	October	10 (cont.), 11, 12
6	November	13, 14
7	December	15, 16
8	January 1877	17, 18
9	February	19

A Woman Hater (cont.)

10	March	20, 21
11	April	22, 23
12	May	24, 25, 26
13	June	27, 28, 29, 30, 31, 32

ᵃPart 2 ends fifty paragraphs short of the end of chapter 5 with "Here's Miss Dover coming, but she is alone."
ᵇPart 4 concludes twenty-one paragraphs short of the end of chapter 10 with "I'll shut the carriage door."

A Woman Hater was published as a volume in June 1877.

Single Heart and Double Face in Life, 8 June–7 September 1882

Part	Date	Chapters in Volume Edition
1ᵃ	8 June 1882	1
2	15 June	2
3	22 June	3ᵇ
4	29 June	3 (cont.), 4ᶜ
5	6 July	4 (cont.)ᵈ
6	13 July	4 (cont.), 5
7	20 July	6
8	27 July	7
9	3 August	8
10	10 August	9
11	17 August	10
12	24 August	11
13	31 August	12ᵉ
14	7 September	12 (cont.)

ᵃThe serial is prefaced with this statement: "Owing to the inefficiency of our present statutes for the protection of literary property, I am compelled to preface this story with a warning that it is a story founded on an original drama, which has been duly performed and registered, so that no heartless thief will be able to take a pair of scissors and drive me off the stage by means of my own dramatic invention snipped out of the columns of LIFE.—CHARLES READE."

ᵇPart 3 ends fifteen paragraphs short of the end of chapter 3 with "his own white dress had suffered by the contact."
ᶜPart 4 ends halfway through chapter 4 with "I will change my coat and join you at the station and bring you back."
ᵈThe serial installment ends with "The man tore his mask off with a snarl of rage: 'I'M THE MASTER OF THE HOUSE!' "
ᵉPart 13 concludes midway through chapter 12 with "Me go to a court of law to part those that were joined till death in a church? That I could never do."

Single Heart and Double Face was published as a volume in July 1884.

A Perilous Secret in *Temple Bar,* September 1884–May 1885

Part	Date	Chapters in Volume Edition
1	September 1884	1, 2, 3, 4
2	October	5, 6, 7, 8
3	November	9, 10, 11, 12
4	December	13, 14
5	January 1885	15, 16, 17
6	February	18, 19, 20, 21
7	March	22, 23
8	April	24, 25
9	May	26, 27

A Perilous Secret was published as a volume on 10 March 1885. It was also published serially in the *Dublin Weekly Freeman* beginning 25 February 1884.

Androgynism in the *English Review,* August–September 1911

Androgynism was published posthumously in the *English Review.* It has never been published as a volume.

Robert Louis Stevenson (1850–94)

Treasure Island "by Captain George North" in *Young Folks*, 1 October 1881–28 January 1882

Part	Date	Chapters in Volume Edition
1	1 October 1881	1, 2
2	8 October	3
3	15 October	4, 5, 6
4	22 October	7, 8, 9
5	29 October	10, 11
6	5 November	12, 13, 14
7	12 November	15, 16
8	19 November	17, 18
9	26 November	19, 20
10	3 December	21, 22
11	10 December	23, 24[a]
12	17 December	24 (cont.), 25, 26
13	24 December	27, 28
14	31 December	29, 30
15	7 January 1882	31
16	14 January	32
17	21 January	33
18	28 January	34

[a]Only the first eighteen paragraphs of chapter 24 are included in part 11.

The Black Arrow "by Captain George North" in *Young Folks*, 30 June–20 October 1883

Part	Date	Chapters in Volume Edition
1	30 June 1883	Prologue
2	7 July	1, 2
3	14 July	3, 4
4	21 July	5, 6

The Black Arrow (cont.)

5	28 July	7; Book 1, Chapter 1
6	4 August	2, 3
7	11 August	4, 5
8	18 August	Book 2, Chapters 1, 2[a]
9	25 August	3, 4
10	1 September	5, 6
11	8 September	Book 3, Chapters 1, 2
12	15 September	3, 4
13	22 September	5, 6
14	29 September	Book 4, Chapters 1, 2
15	6 October	3, 4
16	13 October	5, 6[b]
17	20 October	7, 8

[a]Part 8 ends four paragraphs short of the end of the chapter.
[b]Part 16 ends twenty paragraphs short of the end of the chapter, the last paragraph beginning " 'By the Mass,' said Richard."

The Black Arrow was published as a volume in July 1888.

Prince Otto in Longman's Magazine, April–October 1885

Part	Date	Chapters in Volume Edition
1	April 1885	Book 1, Chapters 1, 2, 3
2	May	4; Book 2, Chapters 1, 2
3	June	3, 4, 5, 6
4	July	7, 8, 9
5	August	10, 11, 12, 13
6	September	14; Book 3, Chapter 1
7	October	2, 3, 4, Bibliographical Postscript

Prince Otto was published as a volume in November 1885.

The Master of Ballantrae in Scribner's Magazine, November 1888–October 1889

Chapters are titled but not numbered in both the serial and the volume.

Part	Date	Chapter Titles in Volume Edition
1	November 1888	"Summary of Events during the Master's Wanderings"[a]
2	December	"Summary of Events" (cont.); "The Master's Wanderings"[b]
3	January 1889	"The Master's Wanderings" (cont.)
4	February	"Persecutions Endured by Mr. Henry"[c]
5	March	"Persecutions Endured by Mr. Henry" (cont.)
6	April	"Account of All That Passed on the Night of February 27th, 1757"
7	May	"Summary of Events during the Master's Second Absence"; "Adventure of Chevalier Burke in India"
8	June	"The Enemy in the House"
9	July	"Mr. Mackellar's Journey with the Master"
10	August	"Passages at New York"
11	September	"The Journey in the Wilderness"[d]
12	October	"The Journey in the Wilderness—Concluded"[d]

[a]Part 1 concludes three quarters of the way through the chapter with the paragraph beginning "Such was the state of this family down to the 7th April, 1749."

[b]Part 2 concludes two thirds of the way through the chapter with the long paragraph beginning "In the meantime our ship was growing very foul" and concluding "each computing what increase had come to his share by the death of the two gunners."

[c]Part 4 ends halfway through the chapter with " 'Ay, Harry, that you may,' said the Master; and I thought Mr. Henry looked at him with a kind of wildness in his eye."

[d]Although using the same title, these are two separate chapters in both the serial and the volume.

The Master of Ballantrae was published as a volume in August 1889.

The Wrecker (written in collaboration with Lloyd Osbourne) in *Scribner's Magazine*, August 1891–July 1892

Part	Date	Chapters in Volume Edition
1	August 1891	Prologue, Chapters 1, 2, 3
2	September	4, 5, 6
3	October	7, 8, 9
4	November	10, 11
5	December	12, 13
6	January 1892	14, 15
7	February	16, 17
8	March	18, 19
9	April	20, 21
10	May	22
11	June	23
12	July	24, 25, Epilogue

The Wrecker was published as a volume in July 1892.

David Balfour: Memoirs of His Adventures at Home and Abroad in *Atalanta*, December 1892–September 1893

English editions of the novel were published under the title *Catriona*.

Part	Date	Chapters in Volume Edition
1	December 1892	Part 1, Chapters 1, 2, 3, 4
2	January 1893	5, 6, 7
3	February	8, 9
4	March	10, 11
5	April	12, 13
6	May	14, 15
7	June	16, 17, 18
8	July	19, 20; Part 2, Chapters 21, 22
9	August	23, 24, 25, 26
10	September	27, 28, 29, 30, Conclusion

David Balfour was published as a volume in September 1893.

The Ebb-Tide (written in collaboration with Lloyd Osbourne) published in *To-Day*, 11 November 1893–3 February 1894

Part	Date	Chapters in Volume Edition
1	11 November 1893	1
2	18 November	2
3	25 November	3
4	2 December	4
5	9 December	5[a]
6	16 December	5 (cont.), 6
7	23 December	7
8	30 December	8
9	6 January 1894	9
10	13 January	10
11	20 January	11[b]
12	27 January	11 (cont.)
13	3 February	12

[a]Part 5 ends two thirds of the way through chapter 5 with the paragraph beginning "The implied last touch completed Herrick's picture of the life and death of his two predecessors. . . . "
[b]Part 11 ends halfway through chapter 11 with "The captain, like a man in a nightmare, laid down his revolver on the table, and Huish wiped the cartridges and oiled the works."

The Ebb-Tide was published as a volume in September 1894.

Weir of Hermiston in *Cosmopolis*, January–April 1896

Part	Date	Chapters in Volume Edition
1[a]	January 1896	Introduction 1, 2
2	February	3, 4, 5
3	March	6
4	April	7, 8, 9

[a]A headnote to part 1 explains that the work is unfinished and posthumous.

Weir of Hermiston was published as a volume on 20 May 1896.

St. Ives in the *Pall Mall Magazine,* November 1896–November 1897

Part	Date	Chapters in Volume Edition
1	November 1896	1, 2, 3
2	December	4, 5, 6
3	January 1897	7, 8, 9
4	February	10, 11, 12
5	March	13, 14, 15
6	April	16, 17, 18
7	May	19, 20, 21
8	June	22, 23, 24
9	July	25, 26, 27
10	August	28, 29, 30ᵃ
11	September	31, 32
12	October	33, 34
13	November	35, 36

ᵃThe following editorial note was appended to the end of part 10: "At this point the story breaks off, having been laid aside by the author some weeks before his death. At the request of the Executors of the Author, Mr. A. T. Quiller-Couch has undertaken to complete the story from the notes furnished by Mrs. Strong, stepdaughter and amanuensis of the late Robert Louis Stevenson. The story will be completed in six chapters, the first installment appearing in the PALL MALL MAGAZINE for September."

William Makepeace Thackeray (1811–63)

Catherine in *Fraser's Magazine,* May 1839–February 1840

Part	Date	Chapters in Volume Edition
1	May 1839	1
2	June	2, 3, 4
3	July	5, 6
4	August	7
5	November	8, 9, 10
6	January 1840	11, 12, 13
7	February	Chapter the Last, Another Last Chapter[a]

[a]The final chapter was considerably reduced from the serial version.

The serial version is reprinted in the Oxford edition (volume 3) and in the Furniss Centenary Edition (volume 6).

The Bedford Row Conspiracy in the *New Monthly Magazine,* January–April 1840

Part	Date	Chapters in Volume Edition
1	January 1840	1
2	March	2
3	April	3

A Shabby Genteel Story in *Fraser's Magazine,* June–October 1840

Part	Date	Chapters in Volume Edition
1	June 1840	1, 2
2	July	3, 4
3	August	5, 6
4	October	7, 8, 9

The story ends abruptly with the October installment. In December Thackeray wrote to Fraser that he had "purposely left the Shabby Genteel Story in such a state that it might be continued in the Magazine or not as you and I liked best." (See Gordon N. Ray, *Thackeray: The Uses of Adversity, 1811–1846* [New York: McGraw-Hill, 1955], p. 235.) Fraser did not take up the offer to continue the work. *The Adventures of Philip* in effect continues *A Shabby Genteel Story.*

The History of Samuel Titmarsh and the Great Hoggarty Diamond in *Fraser's Magazine,* September–December 1841

Part	Date	Chapters in Volume Edition
1	September 1841	1, 2, 3, 4, 5
2	October	6, 7
3	November	8, 9, 10
4	December	11, 12, 13

Fitz-Boodle's Confessions in *Fraser's Magazine,* June, October 1842, January–February 1843

Part	Date	Chapters in Volume Edition
1	June 1842	Preface[a]
2	October	"Miss Lowe"
3	January 1843	"Dorothea"[b]
4	February	"Ottilia," Chapters 1, 2

[a]After serialization the preface was shortened at the end.
[b]In the serial the opening of "Dorothea" contained an additional seven paragraphs.

The Luck of Barry Lyndon: A Romance of the Last Century "by Fitz-Boodle" in Fraser's Magazine, January–December 1844

Part	Date	Chapters in Volume Edition
1	January 1844	1[a]
2	February	2, 3
3	March	4, 5
4	April	6, 7, 8
5	May	9, 10
6	June	11, 12
7	July	13, 14
8	August	15, 16
9	September	17[a]
10	November[b]	18[a]
11	December	19

[a]Barry Lyndon was so poorly received that Thackeray did not publish the novel as a volume until 1856 (although an unauthorized edition was published by the Appleton Company in New York in 1853). Material was omitted from the 1856 edition, the principal omissions being in the middle of the present chapter 1, the beginning of chapter 17, and the end of chapter 18. The volume edition also omits many footnotes that had been introduced to explain ironies in the novel. For a complete list of omissions and revisions see the critical edition, edited by Martin J. Anisman (New York: New York Univ. Press, 1970), which collates the 1844 and 1856 texts.

[b]There was no October installment because Thackeray was on a voyage in the eastern Mediterranean at the time and did not supply copy to the magazine.

The University of Nebraska Press edition (1962) lists the serial parts and reprints passages not included in the Fraser's version; Robert A. Colby in Victorian Fiction: A Second Guide to Research (ed. George H. Ford [New York: MLA, 1978], pp. 121–22) notes that the list of passages is incomplete.

Rebecca and Rowena, published as Proposals for a Continuation of Ivanhoe in Fraser's Magazine, August–September 1846

Rebecca and Rowena was so greatly expanded after the two serial installments that an outline cannot indicate the comparable contents of the two versions. The August part contains, generally, what came to be chapter 1. The September part served as the nucleus for chapters 2–7.

Vanity Fair, twenty parts in nineteen monthly installments, January 1847–July 1848

Part	Date	Chapters in Volume Edition
1	January 1847	1, 2, 3, 4
2	February	5, 6, 7
3	March	8, 9, 10, 11
4	April	12, 13, 14
5	May	15, 16, 17, 18
6	June	19, 20, 21, 22
7	July	23, 24, 25
8	August	26, 27, 28, 29
9	September	30, 31, 32
10	October	33, 34, 35
11	November	36, 37, 38
12	December	39, 40, 41, 42
13	January 1848	43, 44, 45, 46
14	February	47, 48, 49, 50
15	March	51, 52, 53
16	April	54, 55, 56
17	May	57, 58, 59, 60
18	June	61, 62, 63
19–20	July	64, 65, 66, 67

The Riverside and Penguin editions identify the serial parts. The Riverside (ed. Geoffrey Tillotson and Kathleen Tillotson, 1963) also restores some unpublished passages and records variants between printed editions.

Vanity Fair was published as a volume on 18 July 1848. It was also published in two parts in paper wrappers in New York by Harper and Company.

The History of Pendennis, twenty-four parts in twenty-three monthly installments, November 1848–December 1850

Part	Date	Chapters in Volume Edition
1	November 1848	Volume 1, Chapters 1, 2, 3
2	December	4, 5, 6
3	January 1849	7, 8, 9, 10
4	February	11, 12, 13, 14
5	March	15, 16ª, 17
6	April	18ª, 19, 20
7	May	21, 22, 23
8	June	24, 25, 26
9	July	27, 28, 29
10	August	30, 31, 32
11	Septemberᵇ	33, 34, 35, 36
12	January 1850	37, 38
13	February	Volume 2, Chapters 1, 2, 3
14	March	4, 5, 6
15	April	7, 8, 9
16	May	10, 11, 12, 13
17	June	14, 15, 16
18	July	17, 18, 19
19	August	20, 21, 22
20	September	23, 24, 25
21	October	26, 27, 28
22	November	29, 30, 31, 32
23–24	December	33, 34, 35, 36, 37

ªHenry Sayre Van Duzer in *A Thackeray Library* (New York: Burt Franklin, 1971) (p. 99) notes that in the serial volume 1 contained thirty-nine chapters but that in revising for book publication, Thackeray "cut out a portion of Chapter XVI, and a still larger portion of Chapter XVIII, and consolidated the two into one, leaving but thirty-eight chapters in all." It is now believed that Thackeray had nothing to do with these revisions.

ᵇAfter the September 1849 installment publication was suspended for three months because of Thackeray's illness.

The Penguin edition identifies the serial parts.
The History of Pendennis was also published in eight monthly parts in 1849–50 in New York by Harper and Brothers.

The Newcomes, "Edited by Arthur Pendennis," twenty-four parts in twenty-three monthly installments, October 1853–August 1855

Part	Date	Chapters in Volume Edition
1	October 1853	Volume 1, Chapters 1, 2, 3
2	November	4, 5, 6
3	December	7, 8, 9
4	January 1854	10, 11, 12
5	February	13, 14, 15, 16
6	March	17, 18, 19, 20
7	April	21, 22, 23
8	May	24, 25, 26
9	June	27, 28, 29
10	July	30, 31, 32
11	August	33, 34, 35
12	September	36, 37, 38
13	October	Volume 2, Chapters 1, 2, 3
14	November	4, 5, 6
15	December	7, 8, 9
16	January 1855	10, 11, 12, 13
17	February	14, 15, 16
18	March	17, 18, 19
19	April	20, 21, 22, 23
20	May	24, 25, 26, 27
21	June	28, 29, 30, 31
22	July	32, 33, 34, 35
23–24	August	36, 37, 38, 39, 40, 41, 42

The Everyman edition (1962) identifies the serial parts.

The Virginians in twenty-four monthly parts, November 1857–October 1859

Part	Date	Chapters in Volume Edition
1	November 1857	Volume 1, Chapters 1, 2, 3, 4
2	December	5, 6, 7, 8
3	January 1858	9, 10, 11, 12

The Virginians (cont.)

4	February	13, 14, 15, 16
5	March	17, 18, 19, 20
6	April	21, 22, 23, 24
7	May	25, 26, 27, 28
8	June	29, 30, 31, 32
9	July	33, 34, 35, 36
10	August	37, 38, 39, 40
11	September	41, 42, 43, 44
12	October	45, 46, 47, 48
13	November	Volume 2, Chapters 1, 2, 3, 4
14	December	5, 6, 7, 8
15	January 1859	9, 10, 11, 12
16	February	13, 14, 15
17	March	16, 17, 18, 19
18	April	20, 21, 22, 23
19	May	24, 25, 26, 27
20	June	28, 29, 30, 31
21	July	32, 33, 34, 35
22	August	36, 37, 38
23	September	39, 40, 41, 42
24	October	43, 44

The Everyman edition (1961) identifies the serial parts. Also, see Gerald Sorensen, "A Critical Edition of . . . *The Virginians*" (Diss. Minnesota 1966).

Lovel the Widower, published anonymously in the *Cornhill Magazine*, January–June 1860

Part	Date	Chapters in Volume Edition
1	January 1860	1
2	February	2
3	March	3
4	April	4
5	May	5
6	June	6

The Adventures of Philip in the *Cornhill Magazine*, January 1861–August 1862

Part	Date	Chapters in Volume Edition
1	January 1861	Volume 1, Chapters 1, 2, 3
2	February	4, 5
3	March	6, 7
4	April	8, 9, 10
5	May	11, 12
6	June	13, 14
7	July	15, 16
8	August	17, 18
9	September	19, 20
10	October	21, 22
11	November	23; Volume 2, Chapter 1
12	December	2, 3
13	January 1862	4, 5
14	February	6, 7
15	March	8, 9
16	April	10, 11
17	May	12, 13
18	June	14, 15
19	July	16, 17
20	August	18, 19

Denis Duval in the *Cornhill Magazine*, March–June 1864

Part	Date	Chapters in Volume Edition
1	March 1864	1, 2, 3
2	April	4, 5
3	May	6, 7
4	June	8, "Note by the Editor"

This unfinished novel was published posthumously, Thackeray having died on 24 December 1863. The "Note by the Editor" reprints Thackeray's notes for the novel.

Anthony Trollope (1815–82)

Framley Parsonage in the **Cornhill Magazine, January 1860–April 1861**

Part	Date	Chapters in First Edition	Chapters in Two-Volume Edition	Chapters in One-Volume Edition
1	January 1860	Volume 1, Chapters 1, 2, 3	Volume 1, Chapters 1, 2, 3	1, 2, 3
2	February	4, 5, 6	4, 5, 6	4, 5, 6
3	March	7, 8, 9	7, 8, 9	7, 8, 9
4	April	10, 11, 12	10, 11, 12	10, 11, 12
5	May	13, 14, 15	13, 14, 15	13, 14, 15
6	June	16; Volume 2 Chapters 1, 2	16, 17, 18	16, 17, 18
7	July	3, 4, 5	19, 20, 21	19, 20, 21
8	August	6, 7, 8	22, 23, 24	22, 23, 24
9	September	9, 10, 11	Volume 2, Chapters 1, 2, 3	25, 26, 27
10	October	12, 13, 14	4, 5, 6	28, 29, 30
11	November	15; Volume 3, Chapters 1, 2	7, 8, 9	31, 32, 33
12	December	3, 4, 5	10, 11, 12	34, 35, 36
13	January 1861	6, 7, 8	13, 14, 15	37, 38, 39
14	February	9, 10, 11	16, 17, 18	40, 41, 42
15	March	12, 13, 14	19, 20, 21	43, 44, 45
16	April	15, 16, 17	22, 23, 24	46, 47, 48

Framley Parsonage was published as a volume in May 1861.

Orley Farm in twenty monthly parts, March 1861–October 1862

Part	Date	Chapters in First Edition	Chapters in Three-Volume Edition	Chapters in One-Volume Edition
1	March 1861	Volume 1, Chapters 1, 2, 3, 4	Volume 1, Chapters 1, 2, 3, 4	1, 2, 3, 4
2	April	5, 6, 7, 8	5, 6, 7, 8	5, 6, 7, 8
3	May	9, 10, 11, 12	9, 10, 11, 12	9, 10, 11, 12
4	June	13, 14, 15, 16	13, 14, 15, 16	13, 14, 15, 16
5	July	17, 18, 19, 20	17, 18, 19, 20	17, 18, 19, 20
6	August	21, 22, 23, 24	21,22, 23, 24	21, 22, 23, 24
7	September	25, 26, 27, 28	25, 26, 27; Volume 2, Chapter 1	25, 26, 27, 28
8	October	29, 30, 31, 32	2, 3, 4, 5	29, 30, 31, 32
9	November	33, 34, 35, 36	6, 7, 8, 9	33, 34, 35, 36
10	December	37, 38, 39, 40	10, 11, 12, 13	37, 38, 39, 40
11	January 1862	Volume 2, Chapters 1, 2, 3, 4	14, 15, 16, 17	41, 42, 43, 44
12	February	5, 6, 7, 8	18, 19, 20, 21	45, 46, 47, 48
13	March	9, 10, 11, 12	22, 23, 24, 25	49, 50, 51, 52
14	April	13, 14, 15, 16	26, 27; Volume 3, Chapters 1, 2	53, 54, 55, 56
15	May	17, 18, 19, 20	3, 4, 5, 6	57, 58, 59, 60
16	June	21, 22, 23, 24	7, 8, 9, 10	61, 62, 63, 64
17	July	25, 26, 27, 28	11, 12, 13, 14	65, 66, 67, 68
18	August	29, 30, 31, 32	15, 16, 17, 18	69, 70, 71, 72
19	September	33, 34, 35, 36	19, 20, 21, 22	73, 74, 75, 76
20	October	37, 38, 39, 40	23, 24, 25, 26	77, 78, 79, 80

Volume 1 of *Orley Farm* was published in book form on 3 December 1861, volume 2 on 25 September 1862.

The Struggles of Brown, Jones, and Robinson in the *Cornhill* *Magazine*, August 1861–March 1862

Part	Date	Chapters in Volume Edition
1	August 1861	1, 2, 3
2	September	4, 5, 6
3	October	7, 8, 9
4	November	10, 11, 12
5	December	13, 14, 15
6	January 1862	16, 17, 18
7	February	19, 20, 21
8	March	22, 23, 24

The story was not published in England as a volume until 1870, according to Sadleir (p. 48), because of its unpopularity in magazine form.

The Small House at Allington in the *Cornhill Magazine*, September 1862–April 1864

Part	Date	Chapters in First Edition	Chapters in Three-Volume Edition	Chapters in One-Volume Edition
1	September 1862	Volume 1, Chapters 1, 2, 3	Volume 1, Chapters 1, 2, 3	1, 2, 3
2	October	4, 5, 6	4, 5, 6	4, 5, 6
3	November	7, 8, 9	7, 8, 9	7, 8, 9
4	December	10, 11, 12	10, 11, 12	10, 11, 12
5	January 1863	13, 14, 15	13, 14, 15	13, 14, 15
6	February	16, 17, 18	16, 17, 18	16, 17, 18
7	March	19, 20, 21	19, 20; Volume 2, Chapter 1	19, 20, 21
8	April	22, 23, 24	2, 3, 4	22, 23, 24
9	May	25, 26, 27	5, 6, 7	25, 26, 27
10	June	28, 29, 30	8, 9, 10	28, 29, 30
11	July	Volume 2, Chapters 1, 2, 3	11, 12, 13	31, 32, 33

The Small House at Allington (cont.)

12	August	4, 5, 6	14, 15, 16	34, 35, 36
13	September	7, 8, 9	17, 18, 19	37, 38, 39
14	October	10, 11, 12	Volume 3, Chapters 1, 2, 3	40, 41, 42
15	November	13, 14, 15	4, 5, 6	43, 44, 45
16	December	16, 17, 18	7, 8, 9	46, 47, 48
17	January 1864	19, 20, 21	10, 11, 12	49, 50, 51
18	February	22, 23, 24	13, 14, 15	52, 53, 54
19	March	25, 26, 27	16, 17, 18	55, 56, 57
20	April	28, 29, 30	19, 20, 21	58, 59, 60

The Small House at Allington was published as a volume in March 1864.

Can You Forgive Her? in twenty monthly parts, January 1864–August 1865

Part	Date	Chapters in One-Volume Edition	Chapters in Two-Volume Edition	Chapters in Three-Volume Edition
1	January 1864	1, 2, 3, 4	Volume 1, Chapters 1, 2, 3, 4	Volume 1, Chapters 1, 2, 3, 4
2	February	5, 6, 7, 8	5, 6, 7, 8	5, 6, 7, 8
3	March	9, 10, 11, 12	9, 10, 11, 12	9, 10, 11, 12
4	April	13, 14, 15, 16	13, 14, 15, 16	13, 14, 15, 16
5	May	17, 18, 19, 20	17, 18, 19, 20	17, 18, 19, 20
6	June	21, 22, 23, 24	21, 22, 23, 24	21, 22, 23, 24
7	July	25, 26, 27, 28	25, 26, 27, 28	25, 26; Volume 2, Chapters 1, 2
8	August	29, 30, 31, 32	29, 30, 31, 32	3, 4, 5, 6
9	September	33, 34, 35, 36	33, 34, 35, 36	7, 8, 9, 10
10	October	37, 38, 39, 40	37, 38, 39, 40	11, 12, 13, 14
11	November	41, 42, 43, 44	Volume 2, Chapters 1, 2, 3, 4	15, 16, 17, 18

Can You Forgive Her? (cont.)

12	December	45, 46, 47, 48	5, 6, 7, 8	19, 20, 21, 22
13	January 1865	49, 50, 51, 52	9, 10, 11, 12	23, 24, 25, 26
14	February	53, 54, 55, 56	13, 14, 15, 16	Volume 3, Chapters 1, 2, 3, 4
15	March	57, 58, 59, 60	17, 18, 19, 20	5, 6, 7, 8
16	April	61, 62, 63, 64	21, 22, 23, 24	9, 10, 11, 12
17	May	65, 66, 67, 68	25, 26, 27, 28	13, 14, 15, 16
18	June	69, 70, 71, 72	29, 30, 31, 32	17, 18, 19, 20
19	July	73, 74, 75, 76	33, 34, 35, 36	21, 22, 23, 24
20	August	77, 78, 79, 80	37, 38, 39, 40	25, 26, 27, 28

Volume 1 of *Can You Forgive Her?* was published in book form on 1 October 1864, volume 2 in August 1865.

The Belton Estate in the *Fortnightly Review*, 15 May 1865–1 January 1866

Part	Date	Chapters in One-Volume Edition	Chapters in Two-Volume Edition
1	15 May 1865	1, 2	Volume 1, Chapters 1, 2
2	1 June	3, 4	3, 4
3	15 June	5, 6	5, 6
4	1 July	7, 8	7, 8
5	15 July	9, 10	9, 10
6	1 August	11, 12	11, 12
7	15 August	13, 14	13, 14
8	1 September	15, 16	15, 16
9	15 September	17, 18	17; Volume 2, Chapter 1
10	1 October	19, 20	2, 3
11	15 October	21, 22	4, 5
12	1 November	23, 24	6, 7
13	15 November	25, 26	8, 9

The Belton Estate (cont.)

14	1 December	27, 28	10, 11
15	15 December	29, 30	12, 13
16	1 January 1866	31, 32	14, 15

The Belton Estate was published as a volume in January 1866.

The Claverings in the Cornhill Magazine, February 1866–May 1867

Part	Date	Chapters in First Edition	Chapters in One-Volume Edition
1	February 1866	Volume 1, Chapters 1, 2, 3	1, 2, 3
2	March	4, 5, 6ª	4, 5, 6ª
3	April	7, 8, 9	7, 8, 9
4	May	10, 11, 12	10, 11, 12
5	June	13, 14, 15	13, 14, 15
6	July	16, 17, 18	16, 17, 18
7	August	19, 20, 21	19, 20, 21
8	September	22, 23, 24	22, 23, 24
9	October	Volume 2, Chapters 1, 2, 3	25, 26, 27
10	November	4, 5, 6	28, 29, 30
11	December	7, 8, 9	31, 32, 33
12	January 1867	10, 11, 12	34, 35, 36
13	February	13, 14, 15	37, 38, 39
14	March	16, 17, 18	40, 41, 42
15	April	19, 20, 21	43, 44, 45
16	May	22, 23, 24	46, 47, 48

ªChapter 6 in the serial contains six additional paragraphs that were omitted from the volume.

The Dover edition (1977) reproduces the serial version, including the original illustrations.

The Claverings was published as a volume on 20 April 1867.

Nina Balatka in *Blackwood's Magazine,* July 1866–January 1867

Part	Date	Chapters in First Edition	Chapters in One-Volume Edition
1	July 1866	Volume 1, Chapters 1, 2	1, 2
2	August	3, 4, 5	3, 4, 5
3	September	6, 7	6, 7
4	October	8; Volume 2, Chapter 1	8, 9
5	November	2, 3, 4	10, 11, 12
6	December	5, 6	13, 14
7	January 1867	7, 8	15, 16

Nina Balatka was published as a volume on 1 February 1867.

The Last Chronicle of Barset in thirty-two weekly parts, 1 December 1866–6 July 1867

Part	Date	Chapters in First Edition	Chapters in Three-Volume Edition	Chapters in One-Volume Edition
1	1 December 1866	Volume 1, Chapters 1, 2, 3	Volume 1, Chapters 1, 2, 3	1, 2, 3
2	8 December	4, 5, 6	4, 5, 6	4, 5, 6
3	15 December	7, 8	7, 8	7, 8
4	22 December	9, 10, 11	9, 10, 11	9, 10, 11
5	29 December	12, 13, 14	12, 13, 14	12, 13, 14
6	5 January 1867	15, 16	15, 16	15, 16
7	12 January	17, 18, 19	17, 18, 19	17, 18, 19
8	19 January	20, 21, 22	20, 21, 22	20, 21, 22
9	26 January	23, 24	23, 24	23, 24
10	2 February	25, 26, 27	25, 26, 27	25, 26, 27
11	9 February	28, 29, 30, 31	28, 29; Volume 2, Chapters 1, 2	28, 29, 30, 31
12	16 February	32, 33	3, 4	32, 33
13	23 February	34, 35	5, 6	34, 35
14	2 March	36, 37, 38	7, 8, 9	36, 37, 38

The Last Chronicle of Barset (cont.)

15	9 March	39, 40, 41	10, 11, 12	39, 40, 41
16	16 March	42, 43	13, 14	42, 43
17	23 March	Volume 2, Chapters 1, 2, 3	15, 16, 17	44, 45, 46
18	30 March	4, 5	18, 19	47, 48
19	6 April	6, 7	20, 21	49, 50
20	13 April	8, 9	22, 23	51, 52
21	20 April	10, 11, 12	24, 25, 26	53, 54, 55
22	27 April	13, 14	Volume 3, Chapters 1, 2	56, 57
23	4 May	15, 16	3, 4	58, 59
24	11 May	17, 18	5, 6	60, 61
25	18 May	19, 20	7, 8	62, 63
26	25 May	21, 22, 23	9, 10, 11	64, 65, 66
27	1 June	24, 25, 26	12, 13, 14	67, 68, 69
28	8 June	27, 28, 29	15, 16, 17	70, 71, 72
29	15 June	30, 31, 32	18, 19, 20	73, 74, 75
30	22 June	33, 34, 35	21, 22, 23	76, 77, 78
31	29 June	36, 37, 38	24, 25, 26	79, 80, 81
32	6 July	39, 40, 41	27, 28, 29	82, 83, 84

The Penguin edition identifies the end of each serial installment with an asterisk. Volume 1 of *The Last Chronicle of Barset* was published on 16 March 1867, volume 2 on 6 July.

Linda Tressel in *Blackwood's Magazine,* October 1867–May 1868

Part	Date	Chapters in Volume Edition
1	October 1867	1, 2
2	November	3, 4
3	December	5
4	January 1868	6, 7, 8
5	February	9
6	March	10, 11, 12
7	April	13, 14
8	May	15, 16, 17

Linda Tressel was published as a volume in May 1868.

Phineas Finn in *St. Paul's Magazine,* October 1867–May 1869

Part	Date	Chapters in One-Volume Edition	Chapters in Three-Volume Edition
1	October 1867	1, 2, 3, 4	Volume 1, Chapters 1, 2, 3, 4
2	November	5, 6, 7	5, 6, 7
3	December	8, 9, 10, 11	8, 9, 10, 11
4	January 1868	12, 13, 14, 15	12, 13, 14, 15
5	February	16, 17, 18, 19	16, 17, 18, 19
6	March	20, 21, 22, 23	20, 21, 22, 23
7	April	24, 25, 26	24, 25; Volume 2, Chapter 1
8	May	27, 28, 29, 30	2, 3, 4, 5
9	June	31, 32, 33	6, 7, 8
10	July	34, 35, 36, 37	9, 10, 11, 12
11	August	38, 39, 40, 41	13, 14, 15, 16
12	September	42, 43, 44, 45, 46	17, 18, 19, 20, 21
13	October	47, 48, 49, 50	22, 23, 24, 25
14	November	51, 52, 53	26; Volume 3, Chapters 1, 2
15	December	54, 55, 56, 57	3, 4, 5, 6
16	January 1869	58, 59, 60, 61	7, 8, 9, 10
17	February	62, 63, 64	11, 12, 13
18	March	65, 66, 67, 68	14, 15, 16, 17
19	April	69, 70, 71, 72	18, 19, 20, 21
20	May	73, 74, 75, 76	22, 23, 24, 25

Phineas Finn was published as a volume in March 1869.

He Knew He Was Right in thirty-two weekly sixpenny parts, 17 October 1868–22 May 1869

Part	Date	Chapters in Volume Edition
1	17 October 1868	1, 2, 3
2	24 October	4, 5, 6
3	31 October	7, 8, 9
4	7 November	10, 11, 12
5	14 November	13, 14, 15
6	21 November	16, 17, 18
7	28 November	19, 20, 21
8	5 December	22, 23, 24
9	12 December	25, 26, 27
10	19 December	28, 29, 30
11	26 December	31, 32, 33
12	2 January 1869	34, 35, 36
13	9 January	37, 38, 39, 40
14	16 January	41, 42, 43
15	23 January	44, 45, 46
16	30 January	47, 48, 49
17	6 February	50, 51, 52
18	13 February	53, 54, 55
19	20 February	56, 57, 58
20	27 February	59, 60, 61
21	6 March	62, 63, 64
22	13 March	65, 66, 67
23	20 March	68, 69, 70, 71
24	27 March	72, 73, 74
25	3 April	75, 76, 77
26	10 April	78, 79, 80
27	17 April	81, 82, 83
28	24 April	84, 85, 86
29	1 May	87, 88, 89
30	8 May	90, 91, 92
31	15 May	93, 94, 95
32	22 May	96, 97, 98, 99

He Knew He Was Right was published as a volume in May 1869.

The Vicar of Bulhampton in eleven monthly parts, July 1869–May 1870

Part	Date	Chapters in One-Volume Edition	Chapters in Two-Volume Edition
1	July 1869	1, 2, 3, 4, 5, 6, 7	Volume 1, Chapters 1, 2, 3, 4, 5, 6, 7
2	August	8, 9, 10, 11, 12, 13, 14	8, 9, 10, 11, 12, 13, 14
3	September	15, 16, 17, 18, 19, 20	15, 16, 17, 18, 19, 20
4	October	21, 22, 23, 24, 25, 26, 27	21, 22, 23, 24, 25, 26, 27
5	November	28, 29, 30, 31, 32, 33, 34	28, 29, 30, 31, 32, 33, 34
6	December	35, 36, 37, 38, 39, 40, 41	35, 36, 37; Volume 2, Chapters 1, 2, 3, 4
7	January 1870	42, 43, 44, 45	5, 6, 7, 8
8	February	46, 47, 48, 49, 50, 51, 52	9, 10, 11, 12, 13, 14, 15
9	March	53, 54, 55, 56	16, 17, 18, 19
10	April	57, 58, 59, 60, 61, 62, 63, 64	20, 21, 22, 23, 24, 25, 26, 27
11	May	65, 66, 67, 68, 69, 70, 71, 72, 73	28, 29, 30, 31, 32, 33, 34, 35, 36

The Vicar of Bulhampton was published as a volume in April 1870.

Ralph the Heir in supplement to *St. Paul's Magazine,* January 1870–July 1871

Part	Date	Chapters in One-Volume Edition	Chapters in Three-Volume Edition
1	January 1870	1, 2, 3	Volume 1, Chapters 1, 2, 3
2	February	4, 5, 6	4, 5, 6
3	March	7, 8, 9	7, 8, 9
4	April	10, 11, 12	10, 11, 12
5	May	13, 14, 15	13, 14, 15
6	June	16, 17, 18, 19	16, 17, 18, 19
7	July	20, 21, 22	Volume 2, Chapters 1, 2, 3
8	August	23, 24, 25	4, 5, 6

Ralph the Heir (cont.)

9	September	26, 27, 28	7, 8, 9
10	October	29, 30, 31	10, 11, 12
11	November	32, 33, 34	13, 14, 15
12	December	35, 36, 37, 38	16, 17, 18, 19
13	January 1871	39, 40, 41	Volume 3, Chapters 1, 2, 3
14	February	42, 43, 44	4, 5, 6
15	March	45, 46, 47	7, 8, 9
16	April	48, 49	10, 11
17	May	50, 51	12, 13
18	June	52, 53, 54	14, 15, 16
19	July	55, 56, 57, 58	17, 18, 19, 20

Ralph the Heir was published in three volumes on 6 April 1871.

Sir Harry Hotspur in *Macmillan's Magazine,* May–December 1870

Part	Date	Chapters in Volume Edition
1	May 1870	1, 2, 3
2	June	4, 5, 6
3	July	7, 8, 9
4	August	10, 11, 12
5	September	13, 14, 15
6	October	16, 17, 18
7	November	19, 20, 21
8	December	22, 23, 24

Sir Harry Hotspur was published as a volume in November 1870.

The Eustace Diamonds in the *Fortnightly Review*, 1 July 1871–1 February 1873

Part	Date	Chapters in Volume Edition
1	1 July 1871	1, 2, 3, 4
2	1 August	5, 6, 7, 8
3	1 September	9, 10, 11, 12
4	1 October	13, 14, 15, 16
5	1 November	17, 18, 19, 20
6	1 December	21, 22, 23, 24
7	1 January 1872	25, 26, 27, 28
8	1 February	29, 30, 31, 32
9	1 March	33, 34, 35, 36
10	1 April	37, 38, 39, 40
11	1 May	41, 42, 43, 44
12	1 June	45, 46, 47, 48
13	1 July	49, 50, 51, 52
14	1 August	53, 54, 55, 56
15	1 September	57, 58, 59, 60
16	1 October	61, 62, 63, 64
17	1 November	65, 66, 67, 68
18	1 December	69, 70, 71, 72
19	1 January 1873	73, 74, 75, 76
20	1 February	77, 78, 79, 80

The Penguin edition identifies the end of each serial part with three asterisks. *The Eustace Diamonds* was published as a volume in December 1872.

The Golden Lion of Grampere in Good Words, January–August 1872

Part	Date	Chapters in Volume Edition
1	January 1872	1, 2
2	February	3, 4, 5
3	March	6, 7, 8
4	April	9, 10, 11
5	May	12, 13
6	June	14, 15, 16
7	July	17, 18
8	August	19, 20, 21

The Golden Lion of Grampere was published as a volume in May 1872.

Lady Anna in the *Fortnightly Review*, April 1873–April 1874

Part	Date	Chapters in Volume Edition
1	April 1873	1, 2, 3, 4
2	May	5, 6, 7, 8, 9
3	June	10, 11, 12
4	July	13, 14, 15, 16
5	August	17, 18, 19, 20
6	September	21, 22, 23, 24
7	October	25, 26, 27, 28
8	November	29, 30, 31, 32
9	December	33, 34, 35
10	January 1874	36, 37, 38
11	February	39, 40, 41
12	March	42, 43, 44
13	April	45, 46, 47, 48

Lady Anna was published as a volume in May 1874.

Phineas Redux in the *Graphic,* 19 July 1873–10 January 1874

Part	Date	Chapters in First Edition	Chapters in Three-Volume Edition	Chapters in One-Volume Edition
1	19 July 1873	Volume 1, Chapters 1, 2, 3	Volume 1, Chapters 1, 2, 3	1, 2, 3
2	26 July	4, 5, 6	4, 5, 6	4, 5, 6
3	2 August	7, 8, 9	7, 8, 9	7, 8, 9
4	9 August	10, 11, 12	10, 11, 12	10, 11, 12
5	16 August	13, 14, 15	13, 14, 15	13, 14, 15
6	23 August	16, 17, 18	16, 17, 18	16, 17, 18
7	30 August	19, 20, 21	19, 20, 21	19, 20, 21
8	6 September	22, 23, 24	22, 23, 24	22, 23, 24
9	13 September	25, 26, 27	25, 26, 27	25, 26, 27
10	20 September	28, 29, 30	Volume 2, Chapters 1, 2, 3	28, 29, 30
11	27 September	31, 32, 33	4, 5, 6	31, 32, 33
12	4 October	34, 35, 36	7, 8, 9	34, 35, 36
13	11 October	37, 38, 39	10, 11, 12	37, 38, 39
14	18 October	40; Volume 2, Chapters 1, 2	13, 14, 15	40, 41, 42
15	25 October	3, 4, 5	16, 17, 18	43, 44, 45
16	1 November	6, 7, 8	19, 20, 21	46, 47, 48
17	8 November	9, 10, 11	22, 23, 24	49, 50, 51
18	15 November	12, 13, 14	25, 26; Volume 3, Chapter 1	52, 53, 54
19	22 November	15, 16, 17	2, 3, 4	55, 56, 57
20	29 November	18, 19, 20	5, 6, 7	58, 59, 60
21	6 December	21, 22, 23	8, 9, 10	61, 62, 63
22	13 December	24, 25, 26	11, 12, 13	64, 65, 66
23	20 December	27, 28, 29	14, 15, 16	67, 68, 69
24	27 December	30, 31, 32	17, 18, 19	70, 71, 72
25	3 January 1874	33, 34, 35, 36	20, 21, 22, 23	73, 74, 75, 76
26	10 January	37, 38, 39, 40	24, 25, 26, 27	77, 78, 79, 80

Phineas Redux was published as a volume in December 1873.

Harry Heathcote of Gangoil in the *Graphic,* 25 December 1873

Harry Heathcote of Gangoil appeared in its entirety in the Christmas issue of the *Graphic,* 25 December 1873. It was published as a volume in October 1874.

The Way We Live Now in twenty monthly shilling parts, February 1874–September 1875

Part	Date	Chapters in Volume Edition
1	February 1874	1, 2, 3, 4, 5
2	March	6, 7, 8, 9, 10
3	April	11, 12, 13, 14, 15
4	May	16, 17, 18, 19, 20
5	June	21, 22, 23, 24, 25
6	July	26, 27, 28, 29, 30
7	August	31, 32, 33, 34, 35
8	September	36, 37, 38, 39, 40
9	October	41, 42, 43, 44, 45
10	November	46, 47, 48, 49, 50
11	December	51, 52, 53, 54, 55
12	January 1875	56, 57, 58, 59, 60
13	February	61, 62, 63, 64, 65
14	March	66, 67, 68, 69, 70
15	April	71, 72, 73, 74, 75
16	May	76, 77, 78, 79, 80
17	June	81, 82, 83, 84, 85
18	July	86, 87, 88, 89, 90
19	August	91, 92, 93, 94, 95
20	September	96, 97, 98, 99, 100

The Way We Live Now was published as a volume in July 1875.

The Prime Minister in eight monthly parts, November 1875–June 1876

Part	Date	Chapters in One-Volume Edition	Chapters in Three-Volume Edition	Chapters in Four-Volume Edition
1	November 1875	1, 2, 3, 4, 5, 6, 7, 8, 9, 10	Volume 1, Chapters 1, 2, 3, 4, 5, 6, 7, 8, 9, 10	Volume 1, Chapters 1, 2, 3, 4, 5, 6, 7, 8, 9, 10
2	December	11, 12, 13, 14, 15, 16, 17, 18, 19, 20	11, 12, 13, 14, 15, 16, 17, 18, 19, 20	11, 12, 13, 14, 15, 16, 17, 18, 19, 20
3	January 1876	21, 22, 23, 24, 25, 26, 27, 28, 29, 30	21, 22, 23, 24, 25, 26, 27; Volume 2, Chapters 1, 2, 3	Volume 2, Chapters 1, 2, 3, 4, 5, 6, 7, 8, 9, 10
4	February	31, 32, 33, 34, 35, 36, 37, 38, 39, 40	4, 5, 6, 7, 8, 9, 10, 11, 12, 13	11, 12, 13, 14, 15, 16, 17, 18, 19, 20
5	March	41, 42, 43, 44, 45, 46, 47, 48, 49, 50	14, 15, 16, 17, 18, 19, 20, 21, 22, 23	Volume 3, Chapters 1, 2, 3, 4, 5, 6, 7, 8, 9, 10
6	April	51, 52, 53, 54, 55, 56, 57, 58, 59, 60	24, 25, 26; Volume 3, Chapters 1, 2, 3, 4, 5, 6, 7	11, 12, 13, 14, 15, 16, 17, 18, 19, 20
7	May	61, 62, 63, 64, 65, 66, 67, 68, 69, 70	8, 9, 10, 11, 12, 13, 14, 15, 16, 17	Volume 4, Chapters 1, 2, 3, 4, 5, 6, 7, 8, 9, 10
8	June	71, 72, 73, 74, 75, 76, 77, 78, 79, 80	18, 19, 20, 21, 22, 23, 24, 25, 26, 27	11, 12, 13, 14, 15, 16, 17, 18, 19, 20

The Prime Minister was published in book form in May 1876.

The American Senator in *Temple Bar,* May 1876–July 1877

Part	Date	Chapters in First Edition	Chapters in One-Volume Edition
1	May 1876	Volume 1, Chapters 1, 2, 3, 4, 5	1, 2, 3, 4, 5
2	June	6, 7, 8, 9, 10	6, 7, 8, 9, 10
3	July	11, 12, 13, 14, 15	11, 12, 13, 14, 15
4	August	16, 17, 18, 19, 20	16, 17, 18, 19, 20
5	September	21, 22, 23, 24, 25	21, 22, 23, 24, 25
6	October	26, 27; Volume 2, Chapters 1, 2, 3	26, 27, 28, 29, 30
7	November	4, 5, 6, 7, 8	31, 32, 33, 34, 35
8	December	9, 10, 11, 12, 13	36, 37, 38, 39, 40
9	January 1877	14, 15, 16, 17, 18	41, 42, 43, 44, 45
10	February	19, 20, 21, 22, 23	46, 47, 48, 49, 50
11	March	24, 25, 26, 27; Volume 3, Chapter 1	51, 52, 53, 54, 55
12	April	2, 3, 4, 5, 6	56, 57, 58, 59, 60
13	May	7, 8, 9, 10, 11, 12	61, 62, 63, 64, 65, 66
14	June	13, 14, 15, 16, 17, 18, 19	67, 68, 69, 70, 71, 72, 73
15	July	20, 21, 22, 23, 24, 25, 26	74, 75, 76, 77, 78, 79, 80

The American Senator was published in book form in July 1877.

Is He Popenjoy? in *All the Year Round,* 13 October 1877–13 July 1878

Part	Date	Chapters in One-Volume Edition	Chapters in Two-Volume Edition	Chapters in Three-Volume Edition
1	13 October 1877	1	Volume 1, Chapter 1	Volume 1, Chapter 1
2	20 October	2	2	2
3	27 October	3, 4	3, 4	3, 4
4	3 November	5	5	5
5	10 November	6, 7	6, 7	6, 7
6	17 November	8, 9	8, 9	8, 9

Is He Popenjoy? (cont.)

7	24 November	10, 11	10, 11	10, 11
8	1 December	12	12	12
9	8 December	13	13	13
10	15 December	14	14	14
11	22 December	15	15	15
12	29 December	16, 17	16, 17	16, 17
13	5 January 1878	18, 19	18, 19	18, 19
14	12 January	20	20	20
15	19 January	21	21	21
16	26 January	22, 23	22, 23	Volume 2, Chapters 1, 2
17	2 February	24, 25	24, 25	3, 4
18	9 February	26	26	5
19	16 February	27	27	6
20	23 February	28, 29	28, 29	7, 8
21	2 March	30, 31	30, 31	9, 10
22	9 March	32, 33	32; Volume 2, Chapter 1	11, 12
23	16 March	34, 35	2, 3	13, 14
24	23 March	36, 37	4, 5	15, 16
25	30 March	38, 39	6, 7	17, 18
26	6 April	40, 41	8, 9	19, 20
27	13 April	42, 43	10, 11	Volume 3, Chapters 1, 2
28	20 April	44, 45	12, 13	3, 4
29	27 April	46, 47	14, 15	5, 6
30	4 May	48, 49	16, 17	7, 8
31	11 May	50	18	9
32	18 May	51, 52	19, 20	10, 11
33	25 May	53, 54	21, 22	12, 13
34	1 June	55, 56	23, 24	14, 15
35	8 June	57, 58	25, 26	16, 17
36	15 June	59	27	18
37	22 June	60	28	19
38	29 June	61	29	20
39	6 July	62, 63	30, 31	21, 22
40	13 July	64	32	23

Is He Popenjoy? was published in book form in April 1878.

John Caldigate in *Blackwood's Magazine*, April 1878–June 1879

Part	Date	Chapters in First Edition	Chapters in Two-Volume Edition	Chapters in One-Volume Edition
1	April 1878	Volume 1, Chapters 1, 2, 3, 4	Volume 1, Chapters 1, 2, 3, 4	1, 2, 3, 4
2	May	5, 6, 7, 8	5, 6, 7, 8	5, 6, 7, 8
3	June	9, 10, 11, 12	9, 10, 11, 12	9, 10, 11, 12
4	July	13, 14, 15, 16	13, 14, 15, 16	13, 14, 15, 16
5	August	17, 18, 19, 20	17, 18, 19, 20	17, 18, 19, 20
6	September	21; Volume 2, Chapters 1, 2, 3	21, 22, 23, 24	21, 22, 23, 24
7	October	4, 5, 6, 7	25, 26, 27, 28	25, 26, 27, 28
8	November	8, 9, 10, 11	29, 30, 31, 32	29, 30, 31, 32
9	December	12, 13, 14, 15	Volume 2, Chapters 1, 2, 3, 4	33, 34, 35, 36
10	January 1879	16, 17, 18, 19	5, 6, 7, 8	37, 38, 39, 40
11	February	20, 21; Volume 3, Chapters 1, 2, 3	9, 10, 11, 12, 13	41, 42, 43, 44, 45
12	March	4, 5, 6, 7, 8	14, 15, 16, 17, 18	46, 47, 48, 49, 50
13	April	9, 10, 11, 12	19, 20, 21, 22	51, 52, 53, 54
14	May	13, 14, 15, 16, 17	23, 24, 25, 26, 27	55, 56, 57, 58, 59
15	June	18, 19, 20, 21, 22	28, 29, 30, 31, 32	60, 61, 62, 63, 64

John Caldigate was published in book form in June 1879.

An Eye for an Eye in the Whitehall Review, 24 August 1878– 1 February 1879

Part	Date	Chapters in First Edition	Chapters in One-Volume Edition
1	24 August 1878	Introduction; Book 1, Chapter 1	1
2	31 August	2	2
3	7 September	3	3
4	14 September	4	4
5	21 September	5[a]	5[a]
6	28 September	5 (cont.), 6	5 (cont.), 6
7	5 October	7	7
8	12 October	8	8
9	19 October	9	9
10	26 October	10	10
11	2 November	11	11
12	9 November	12	12
13	16 November	Book 2, Chapter 1	13
14	23 November	2	14
15	30 November	3	15
16	7 December	4	16
17	14 December	5	17
18	21 December	6	18
19	28 December	7	19
20	4 January 1879	8	20
21	11 January	9	21
22	18 January	10	22
23	25 January	11	23
24	1 February	12	24

[a]Part 5 ends six paragraphs short of the end of chapter 5 with "That eternity is coming, with all its glory and happiness. If it were not so, it would, indeed, be very bad."

An Eye for an Eye was published in book form in January 1879.

Cousin Henry in supplement to the *Manchester Weekly Times,* 8 March–24 May 1879

Part	Date	Chapters in First Edition	Chapters in One-Volume Edition
1	8 March 1879	Book 1, Chapters 1, 2	1, 2
2	15 March	3, 4	3, 4
3	22 March	5, 6	5, 6
4	29 March	7, 8	7, 8
5	5 April	9, 10	9, 10
6	12 April	11, 12	11, 12
7	19 April	Book 2, Chapters 1, 2	13, 14
8	26 April	3, 4	15, 16
9	3 May	5, 6	17, 18
10	10 May	7, 8	19, 20
11	17 May	9, 10	21, 22
12	24 May	11, 12	23, 24

Cousin Henry was published in book form in November 1879.

The Duke's Children in *All the Year Round,* 4 October 1879–24 July 1880

Part	Date	Chapters in Three-Volume Edition	Chapters in One-Volume Edition
1	4 October 1879	Volume 1, Chapters 1, 2	1, 2
2	11 October	3, 4	3, 4
3	18 October	5, 6	5, 6
4	25 October	7	7
5	1 November	8, 9	8, 9
6	8 November	10, 11	10, 11
7	15 November	12, 13	12, 13
8	22 November	14	14

The Duke's Children (cont.)

9	29 November	15, 16	15, 16
10	6 December	17, 18	17, 18
11	13 December	19, 20	19, 20
12	20 December	21, 22	21, 22
13	27 December	23, 24	23, 24
14	3 January 1880	25	25
15	10 January	26; Volume 2, Chapter 1	26, 27
16	17 January	2, 3	28, 29
17	24 January	4, 5	30, 31
18	31 January	6	32
19	7 February	7, 8	33, 34
20	14 February	9, 10	35, 36
21	21 February	11, 12	37, 38
22	28 February	13, 14	39, 40
23	6 March	15, 16	41, 42
24	13 March	17, 18	43, 44
25	20 March	19, 20	45, 46
26	27 March	21, 22	47, 48
27	3 April	23, 24	49, 50
28	10 April	25, 26	51, 52
29	17 April	27; Volume 3, Chapter 1	53, 54
30	24 April	2, 3	55, 56
31	1 May	4, 5	57, 58
32	8 May	6	59
33	15 May	7, 8	60, 61
34	22 May	9, 10	62, 63
35	29 May	11, 12	64, 65
36	5 June	13, 14	66, 67
37	12 June	15, 16	68, 69
38	19 June	17, 18	70, 71
39	26 June	19, 20	72, 73
40	3 July	21, 22	74, 75
41	10 July	23	76
42	17 July	24	77
43	24 July	25, 26, 27	78, 79, 80

The Duke's Children was published in book form in May 1880.

Dr. Wortle's School in Blackwood's Magazine, May–December 1880

Part	Date	Chapters in First Edition	Chapters in One-Volume Edition
1	May 1880	Volume 1, Chapters 1, 2, 3	1, 2, 3
2	June	4, 5, 6	4, 5, 6
3	July	7, 8, 9	7, 8, 9
4	August	10, 11, 12	10, 11, 12
5	September	Volume 2, Chapters 1, 2, 3	13, 14, 15
6	October	4, 5, 6	16, 17, 18
7	November	7, 8, 9	19, 20, 21
8	December	10, 11, 12	22, 23, 24

Dr. Wortle's School was published in book form in February 1881.

The Fixed Period in Blackwood's Magazine, October 1881–March 1882

Part	Date	Chapters in Volume Edition
1	October 1881	1, 2
2	November	3, 4
3	December	5, 6
4	January 1882	7, 8
5	February	9, 10
6	March	11, 12

Marion Fay in the Graphic, 3 December 1881–3 June 1882

Part	Date	Chapters in One-Volume Edition	Chapters in Three-Volume Edition
1	3 December 1881	1, 2	Volume 1, Chapters 1, 2
2	10 December	3, 4	3, 4
3	17 December	5, 6	5, 6
4	24 December	7, 8	7, 8

Marion Fay (cont.)

5	31 December	9, 10	9, 10
6	7 January 1882	11, 12	11, 12
7	14 January	13, 14	13, 14
8	21 January	15, 16	15, 16
9	28 January	17, 18	17, 18
10	4 February	19, 20	19, 20
11	11 February	21, 22	21, 22
12	18 February	23, 24	Volume 2, Chapters 1, 2
13	25 February	25, 26	3, 4
14	4 March	27, 28	5, 6
15	11 March	29, 30, 31	7, 8, 9
16	18 March	32, 33, 34	10, 11, 12
17	1 April	35, 36, 37	13, 14, 15
18	8 April	38, 39, 40	16, 17, 18
19	15 April	41, 42, 43	19, 20, 21
20	22 April	44, 45, 46	Volume 3, Chapters 1, 2, 3
21	29 April	47, 48, 49	4, 5, 6
22	6 May	50, 51, 52	7, 8, 9
23	13 May	53, 54, 55	10, 11, 12
24	20 May	56, 57, 58	13, 14, 15
25	27 May	59, 60, 61	16, 17, 18
26	3 June	62, 63, 64	19, 20, 21

Marion Fay was published in book form in May 1882.

Kept in the Dark in *Good Words,* May–December 1882

Part	Date	Chapters in Volume Edition
1	May 1882	1, 2, 3
2	June	4, 5, 6
3	July	7, 8, 9
4	August	10, 11, 12
5	September	13, 14, 15

Kept in the Dark (cont.)

6	October	16, 17, 18
7	November	19, 20, 21
8	December	22, 23, 24

Kept in the Dark was published in book form in October 1882.

Mr. Scarborough's Family in All the Year Round, 27 May 1882–16 June 1883

Part	Date	Chapters in Volume Edition
1	27 May 1882	1, 2
2	3 June	3, 4
3	10 June	5
4	17 June	6, 7
5	24 June	8, 9
6	1 July	10
7	8 July	11
8	15 July	12, 13
9	22 July	14, 15
10	29 July	16
11	5 August	17, 18
12	12 August	19
13	19 August	20
14	26 August	21
15	2 September	22
16	9 September	23, 24
17	16 September	25
18	23 September	26
19	30 September	27
20	7 October	28
21	14 October	29
22	21 October	30
23	28 October	31
24	4 November	32

Mr. Scarborough's Family (cont.)

25	11 November	33
26	18 November	34
27	25 November	35
28	2 December	36
29	9 December	37
30	16 December	38
31	23 December	39[a]
32	30 December	40
33	6 January 1883	41
34	13 January	42
35	20 January	43
36	27 January	44
37	3 February	45
38	10 February	46
39	17 February	47
40	24 February	48
41	3 March	49
42	10 March	50
43	17 March	51
44	24 March	52
45	31 March	53
46	7 April	54
47	14 April	55
48	21 April	56
49	28 April	57
50	5 May	58
51	12 May	59
52	19 May	60
53	26 May	61
54	2 June	62
55	9 June	63
56	16 June	64

[a]The following note is attached to the end of part 31: "The lamentable death of Mr. Anthony Trollope will not in any way interfere with the continuation of 'Mr. Scarborough's Family.' The story was completed, and in the hands of the printer, some months ago."

Mr. Scarborough's Family was published in book form in May 1883.

The Landleaguers in *Life,* 16 November 1882–4 October 1883

Part	Date	Chapters in Volume Edition
1	16 November 1882	1, 2
2	23 November	3
3	30 November	4
4	7 December	5
5	14 December	Obituary of Trollope, Chapters 1–5 reprinted, plus Chapter 6
6	21 December	7, 8
7	28 December	9
8	4 January 1883	10, 11
9	11 January	12
10	18 January	13
11	25 January	14
12	1 February	15
13	8 February	16
14	15 February	17
15	22 February	18
16	1 March	19
17	8 March	20
18	15 March	21
19	22 March	22
20	29 March	23
21	5 April	24
22	12 April	25
23	19 April	26[a]
24	26 April	26 (cont.), 27
25	3 May	28
26	10 May	29
27	17 May	30
28	24 May	31
29	31 May	32
30	7 June	33
31	14 June	34
32	21 June	35
33	28 June	36
34	5 July	37
35	12 July	38

The Landleaguers (cont.)

36	19 July	39
37	26 July	40
38	2 August	41[b]
39	9 August	41 (cont.), 42[c]
40	16 August	42 (cont.), 43[d]
41	23 August	43 (cont.)
42	30 August	44
43	6 September	45
44	13 September	46
45	20 September	47
46	27 September	48
47	4 October	49, with note appended by Trollope's son, Henry M. Trollope

[a]Part 23 concludes just short of end of chapter 26 with "Well yes; M. Le Gros explained that the proposition was not *selon les regles*, and it does not matter the least in the world."

[b]Part 38 ends just past the middle of chapter 41 with the paragraph beginning "But on estates where the Commissioners are allowed their full swing, the whole nature of the property in the land will be altered."

[c]Part 39 ends with the paragraph beginning "It was now far advanced in May, and Mr. O'Mahoney had resolved to make one crushing eloquent speech in the House of Commons and then to retire to the United States."

[d]Only the first six paragraphs of chapter 43 are included.

The Landleaguers was published in book form in October 1883.

Mrs. Humphry Ward (Mary Augusta Ward, née Arnold) (1851–1920)

The Story of Bessie Costrell in the Cornhill Magazine, May–July 1895

Part	Date	Chapters in Volume Edition
1	May 1895	1, 2, 3
2	June	4
3	July	5

The Story of Bessie Costrell was published in book form in July 1895.

Sir George Thessady in Century Magazine, November 1895–October 1896

Part	Date	Chapters in Volume Edition
1	November 1895	1, 2
2	December	3, 4
3	January 1896	5, 6[a]
4	February	7, 8
5	March	9
6	April	10, 11, 12
7	May	13, 14[b]
8	June	15, 16
9	July	17, 18
10	August	19, 20
11	September	21, 22
12	October	23, 24

[a]Chapter 6 concluded with the paragraph beginning "After another pensive turn or two she stopped beside a photograph that stood upon her writing-table." The additional twenty-five paragraphs were added for the volume edition.
[b]The first five paragraphs of chapter 14 were added after serialization.

Sir George Thessady was published in book form in September 1896.

Eleanor in *Harper's New Monthly Magazine,* January–December 1900

Part	Date	Chapters in Volume Edition
1	January 1900	1, 2
2	February	3, 4
3	March	5, 6
4	April	7, 8
5	May	9, 10
6	June	11, 12
7	July	13, 14
8	August	15, 16
9	September	17, 18
10	October	19, 20
11	November	21, 22, 23[a]
12	December	23 (cont.), 24, 25

[a]Part 11 ends two thirds through chapter 23 with " 'Avanti!' cried the coachman, and the horses began to toil sleepily up the hill."

Eleanor was published in book form in November 1900.

Lady Rose's Daughter in *Harper's Monthly Magazine,* May 1902–April 1903

Part	Date	Chapters in Volume Edition
1	May 1902	1, 2
2	June	3, 4
3	July	5, 6
4	August	7, 8
5	September	9, 10
6	October	11, 12
7	November	13, 14
8	December	15, 16
9	January 1903	17, 18
10	February	19, 20
11	March	21, 22
12	April	23, 24

Lady Rose's Daughter was published in book form in March 1903.

The Testing of Diana Mallory in *Harper's Magazine,* November 1907– October 1908

Part	Date	Chapters in Volume Edition
1	November 1907	1, 2
2	December	3, 4
3	January 1908	5, 6
4	February	7, 8
5	March	9, 10
6	April	11, 12
7	May	13, 14
8	June	15, 16
9	July	17, 18
10	August	19, 20
11	September	21, 22
12	October	23, 24

The Testing of Diana Mallory was published in book form in September 1908.

Daphne; or, Marriage à la Mode, published as *Marriage à la Mode,* in the *Pall Mall Magazine,* January–June 1909

Part	Date	Chapters in Volume Edition
1	January 1909	1, 2
2	February	3, 4
3	March	5[a], 6
4	April	7, 8
5	May	9, 10
6	June	11, 12

[a]Chapter 5 was expanded by about one third after serialization.

Daphne was also serialized in *McClure's Magazine,* January–June 1909. It was published in book form in May 1909.

Notes on Periodicals

Ainsworth's Magazine, February 1842–December 1854. William Harrison Ainsworth was the founding editor but not the proprietor. See S. M. Ellis, *William Harrison Ainsworth and His Friends* (London: John Lane, 1911).

All the Year Round, April 1859–April 1895. A weekly magazine founded by Charles Dickens.

Argosy, a London monthly, December 1865–December 1901, was subtitled *A Magazine of Tales, Travels, Essays and Poems.* It was edited by Mrs. Henry Wood from its founding until June 1887.

Atlantic Monthly, subtitled *A Magazine of Literature, Art, and Politics,* began publication in November 1857 in Boston.

Atalanta, a London monthly, October 1887–September 1898. It was edited by L. T. Meads and A. B. Symington during the serialization of Stevenson's *Catriona (David Balfour).*

Belgravia, a London monthly, November 1866–June 1899, edited by M. E. Braddon from 1866 to 1893.

Bentley's Miscellany, January 1837–December 1868. Dickens was editor 1837–39; William Harrison Ainsworth 1839–41.

Blackwood's Edinburgh Magazine, founded in 1817; after January 1907 the title was *Blackwood's Magazine.* See Margaret Oliphant, *Annals of a Publishing House: William Blackwood and His Sons—Their Magazine and Friends* (New York, 1897).

Bolton Weekly Journal, a London newspaper, founded 1871.

Bow Bells, a London weekly magazine, 12 November 1862–15 March 1897. It was subtitled *A Weekly Magazine of General Literature and Art, for Family Reading.*

Canadian Monthly, published in Toronto, January 1872–June 1882.

Cassell's Magazine carried this title from 1867 to 1874. It had earlier been *Cassell's Illustrated Family Paper* and was later variously published as *Cassell's Magazine, Cassell's Family Magazine,* and *Cassell's Magazine of Fiction.*

Century, a quarterly, was published in New York, November 1870–May 1930.

Cosmopolis, a London monthly, January 1896–November 1898.

Cornhill, founded January 1860. Thackeray was the founding editor and continued until May 1862. Because it was a success as a quality low-priced magazine, the *Cornhill* inspired a number of imitators. See the *Wellesley Index to Victorian Periodicals,* I, 321–24.

English Review, a London monthly, December 1908–July 1937.

Era, a London newspaper, 30 September 1838–21 September 1839.

Fortnightly Review, London, May 1865–December 1954, was published twice monthly through 15 October 1866, then monthly. See Edwin

M. Everett, *The Party of Humanity:* The Fortnightly Review *and Its Contributors, 1865–1874* (Chapel Hill: Univ. of North Carolina Press, 1939). See also the *Wellesley Index*, II, 173–83.

Fraser's Magazine, a London monthly, February 1830–October 1882. See Miriam M. H. Thrall, *Rebellious Fraser's: Nol Yorke's Magazine in the Days of Maginn, Thackeray, and Carlyle* (New York: Columbia Univ. Press, 1934). See also the *Wellesley Index*, II, 303–19.

Glasgow Weekly Herald, a newspaper, began publishing 12 November 1864.

Good Words, an Edinburgh monthly family magazine with a religious bent, frequently carried sermons and inspirational essays. It was founded in January 1860 under the editorship of Norman Macleod. In May 1906 it was amalgamated with the *Sunday Magazine* and was issued as a weekly paper in London.

The Graphic, an illustrated weekly London newspaper, was founded in 1869. In 1932 it became the *National Graphic.*

Harper's New Monthly Magazine began publication in 1850; in 1900 the title became *Harper's Monthly Magazine,* in 1925 *Harper's Magazine.*

Home Companion, a London magazine, was published from 1852 to 1854.

Household Words, a weekly family magazine founded by Charles Dickens, was published from 30 March 1850 to 28 May 1859. See Anne Lohrli, Household Words: *A Weekly Journal 1850–1859 Conducted by Charles Dickens* (Toronto: Univ. of Toronto Press, 1973).

Illustrated London News, a weekly newspaper begun 14 May 1842 and still publishing.

Leigh Journal and Times, a weekly newspaper published at Leigh, Lancaster, beginning 6 June 1874, and still in publication.

Life, a London weekly newspaper, published 12 July 1879–15 December 1906.

Lippincott's Monthly Magazine was the English edition of *Lippincott's Magazine of Literature, Science, and Education,* founded in Philadelphia in January 1868.

London Journal and Weekly Record of Literature, Science, and Art was a weekly newspaper, 1845–1906.

London Society, a monthly magazine, February 1862–December 1898, contained fiction and general literature.

Longman's Magazine, a monthly magazine published in London, 1882–1905. See Cyprian Blagden, *"Longman's Magazine," Review of English Literature,* 4 (1963), 9–22.

McClure's Magazine, a New York monthly, 1893–1929, published fiction and general literature.

Macmillan's Magazine, a London monthly, November 1859–November 1907. See John Collins Francis, "Macmillan's Magazine," *Notes and Queries* 11th ser., 1 (1910), 141–42; "One Hundred Years of Macmillan

History," *Publisher's Weekly*, 9 October 1943, pp. 1430–38; *Wellesley Index*, I, 554–56.

Manchester Weekly Times began publication on 23 June 1855 as the **Manchester Weekly Examiner and Times.**

Metropolitan Magazine, subtitled *A Monthly Journal of Literature, Science and the Fine Arts,* was founded in London in 1831 and continued until 1855.

New Monthly Magazine began publication in 1814. It gained prominence after 1821 under the editorship of Thomas Campbell. Later editors included Bulwer-Lytton, Theodore Hook, Thomas Hood, and William Harrison Ainsworth. See *Wellesley Index*, III, 161–72.

Once a Week, a London weekly "illustrated miscellany," was published from 1859 to 1880.

Pearson's Magazine, 1896–1939, was a monthly aimed primarily at young readers.

Pall Mall Magazine, founded in 1893, was a general literature magazine.

St. Paul's, a monthly magazine, first appeared in October 1867 with Anthony Trollope as the founding editor. See *Wellesley Index*, III, 358–64.

Sunday Times was founded in 1821 as the **Independent Observer** and changed its name during the next year. See Harold Hobson, Phillip Knightly, and Leonard Russell eds., *The Pearl of Days: An Intimate Memoir of the Sunday Times, 1822–1972* (London: H. Hamilton, 1972).

Temple Bar, a London monthly magazine of general literature. George Augusta Sala was the first editor. See *Wellesley Index*, III, 386–91.

Tinsley's Magazine, a London monthly founded in 1867 under the editorship of Edmund Yates.

To-Day, a London weekly newspaper, founded in 1893.

Whitehall Review, a London weekly newspaper, founded in 1876.

World, a London weekly newspaper, begun in 1874.

Young Folks, a London weekly newspaper, first published in 1871 as **Our Young Folk's** [sic] **Budget.**

Selected Bibliography

GENERAL

Altick, Richard D. *The English Common Reader: A Social History of the Mass Reading Public, 1800–1900.* Chicago: Univ. of Chicago Press, 1957.

Carter, John. "Nineteenth Century Books: Some Bibliographical Agenda." In his *Books and Book-Collectors.* Cleveland: World, 1957, pp. 157–86.

Dickson, Sarah. *A Checklist of the Arents Collection of Books in Parts and Associated Literature.* New York: New York Public Library, 1957.

Fader, Daniel. *The Periodical Context of English Literature, 1708–1907.* Ann Arbor: University Microfilms, 1971.

Keech, James M. "Three-Deckers and Installment Novels: The Effect of Publishing Format upon the Nineteenth-Century Novel." *DA,* 26 (1966), 4631A (Louisiana State).

Lund, Michael. "Clocking the Reader in the Long Victorian Novel." *Victorian Newsletter,* No. 59 (1981), pp. 22–25.

Pollard, Graham. "Novels in Newspapers." *Review of English Studies,* 18 (1942), 72–85.

———. "Serial Fiction," In *New Paths in Book Collecting.* Ed. John Carter. London: Constable, 1934, pp. 247–77.

Sutherland, John A. *Victorian Novelists and Publishers.* Chicago: Univ. of Chicago Press; London: Althone, 1976.

Tiemersma, Richard R. "Fiction in the *Cornhill Magazine,* January 1860–March 1871." *DA,* 23 (1963), 3358 (Northwestern).

Tillotson, Kathleen. *Novels of the Eighteen-Forties.* London: Oxford Univ. Press, 1954.

Wellesley Index to Victorian Periodicals. Ed. Walter E. Houghton. 3 vols. Toronto: Univ. of Toronto Press, 1966–79.

Wiles, R. M. *Serial Publication in England before 1750.* Cambridge: Cambridge Univ. Press, 1957.

INDIVIDUAL AUTHORS

Collins

Seiter, Richard D. "Wilkie Collins as Writer for Charles Dickens's *Household Words* (1850–1859) and *All the Year Round* (1859–1870)." *DA,* 31 (1970), 1771A (Bowling Green State).

Sutherland, John. "Two Emergencies in the Writing of *The Woman in White.*" *Yearbook of English Studies,* 7 (1977) 148–56.

Dickens

Axton, William. "Keystone Structure in Dickens' Serial Novels." *University of Toronto Quarterly,* 37 (1967), 31–50.

Belmont, Anthony M., Jr. "An Analysis of the Structure of the Chapters and Serial Divisions of Charles Dickens's *Bleak House.*" *DAI,* 40 (1979), 1478A (Arkansas).

Blasky, Andrew H. "Once a Month, All the Year Round: The English Serial Novel." *DAI,* 39 (1978), 890A (Berkeley).

Butt, John. "The Serial Publication of Dickens' Novels: *Martin Chuzzlewit* and *Little Dorrit.*" In his *Pope, Dickens, and Others.* Edinburgh: Edinburgh Univ. Press, 1969.

———, and Kathleen Tillotson. *Dickens at Work.* London: Methuen, 1957.

Casey, Ellen M. "Novels in Teaspoonfuls: Serial Novels in *All the Year Round.*" *DA,* 30 (1969), 1521A (Wisconsin).

Churchill, R. C. "The Monthly Dickens and the Weekly Dickens." *Contemporary Review,* 234 (Feb. 1979), 97–101.

Coolidge, Archibald C. *Charles Dickens as a Serial Novelist.* Ames: Iowa State Univ. Press, 1967.

Easson, Angus. "*The Old Curiosity Shop*: From Manuscript to Print." *Dickens Studies Annual,* 1 (1970), 93–128.

Fielding, K. J. "Dickens as Serial Novelist." *Dickensian,* 63 (1961), 156–57.

———. "The Monthly Serialization of Dickens's Novels." *Dickensian,* 54 (1958), 4–11.

———. "The Weekly Serialization of Dickens's Novels." *Dickensian,* 54 (1958), 134–41.

Genet, George M. "Charles Dickens and the Magazine World: The Periodical Author in the Eighteen Thirties." *DAI,* 37 (1976), 330A (Berkeley).

Grubb, G. G. "Dickens's Pattern of Weekly Serialization." *Journal of English Literary History,* 4 (1942), 141–56.

———. "On the Serial Publication of *Oliver Twist.*" *Modern Language Notes,* 56 (1941), 290–94.

Harvey, J. R. "The Concern of Serial Novelists with the Illustrations of Their Work in the Nineteenth Century with Particular Reference to Dickens." Diss. Cambridge 1969.

Herring, Paul D. "Dickens's Monthly Number Plans for *Little Dorrit.*" *Modern Philology,* 64 (1966), 22–63.

Levy, Herman M., Jr. "Dickens and the Novel in Parts." *DA,* 27 (1966), 478A (Western Reserve).

Monod, Sylvère. "Dickens at Work on the Text of *Hard Times.*" *Dickensian,* 64 (1968), 86–99.

Patten, Robert. *Charles Dickens and His Publishers.* Oxford: Clarendon, 1975.

———. "*Pickwick Papers* and the Development of Serial Fiction." *Rice University Studies,* 61 (1975), 51–74.

Savage, Robert B. "Artist-Audience Collaboration in Dickens' Serials." *DA,* 37 (1976), 3650A (Ohio).

Schachterle, Lance. "*Bleak House* as a Serial Novel." *Dickens Studies Annual,* 1 (1970), 212–24.

———. "Charles Dickens and the Techniques of the Serial Novel." *DA,* 31 (1971), 5424A (Pennsylvania).

———. "*Oliver Twist* and Its Serial Predecessors." *Dickens Studies Annual,* 3 (1974), 1–13.

Smith, Harry B. "How Charles Dickens Wrote His Books." *Harper's Magazine,* 150 (Dec. 1924), 50–60.

Sucksmith, H. P. "Dickens at Work on *Bleak House*: A Critical Examination of His Memoranda and Number Plans." *Renaissance and Modern Studies*, 9 (1966), 47–85.

Eliot

Beaty, Jerome. Middlemarch *from Notebook to Novel*. Urbana: Univ. of Illinois Press, 1960.

Kitchel, Anna T., ed. *Quarry for* Middlemarch. Berkeley: Univ. of California Press; London: Cambridge Univ. Press, 1950.

Gaskell

Carwell, Virginia A. "Serialization and the Fiction of Mrs. Gaskell." *DA*, 26 (1965), 3328A.

Collin, Dorothy W. "The Composition of Mrs. Gaskell's *North and South.*" *Bulletin of John Rylands Library*, 54 (1971), 67–93.

Hopkins, Annette B. "Dickens and Mrs. Gaskell." *Huntington Library Quarterly*, 9, (1946), 357–85.

Hardy

"Adventures of a Novel: *Tess* after Fifty Years." *Times Literary Supplement*, 5 July 1941, p. 322.

Chase, Mary Ellen. *Thomas Hardy from Serial to Novel*. Minneapolis: Univ. of Minnesota Press, 1927.

Jones, Lawrence O. "*Desperate Remedies* and the Victorian Sensation Novel." *Nineteenth-Century Fiction*, 20 (1965), 35–50.

———. " 'A Good Hand at a Serial': Thomas Hardy and the Serialization of *Far from the Madding Crowd.*" *Studies in the Novel*, 10 (1978), 320–24.

Laird, J. T. "New Light on the Evolution of *Tess of the D'Urbervilles.*" *Review of English Studies*, 31 (1980), 414–35.

———. *The Shaping of* Tess of the D'Urbervilles. Oxford: Clarendon, 1975.

Page, Norman. "Hardy's 'The Midnight Baptism.' " *Colby Library Quarterly*, 9 (1972), 582–85.

Paterson, John. *The Making of* The Return of the Native. Berkeley: Univ. of California Press, 1960.

Peterson, Audrey C. " 'A Good Hand at a Serial': Thomas Hardy and the Art of Fiction." *Victorian Newsletter*, No. 46 (Fall 1974), pp. 24–26.

Purdy, R. L. "Manuscript Adventures of *Tess.*" *Times Literary Supplement*, 6 March 1943, p. 120; 26 June 1943, p. 307.

Slack, Robert C. "The Text of Hardy's *Jude the Obscure.*" *Nineteenth-Century Fiction*, 11 (1957), 251–75.

Ward, Paul. "*Desperate Remedies* and the Victorian Thriller." *Thomas Hardy Yearbook*, 4 (1973–74), 72–76.

Kingsley

Scott, P. G. and Larry K. Uffelman. "Kingsley's Serial Novels: *Yeast.*" *Victorian Periodicals Newsletter*, 9 (1976), 111–19.

Meredith

Beer, Gillian. "Meredith's Revisions of *The Tragic Comedians*." *Review of English Studies*, NS 14 (1963), 33–53.

Cotton, Jo Ray. "*Evan Harrington*: An Analysis of George Meredith's Revisions." *DA*, 29 (1968), 895A–96A (Southern California).

Gettman, R. A. "Serialization and *Evan Harrington*." *PMLA*, 64 (1949), 963–75.

Hergenhan, L. T. "Meredith's Revisions of *Harry Richmond*." *Review of English Studies*, NS 14 (1963), 24–32.

Measures, Joyce E. "Meredith's *Diana of the Crossways*: Revisions and Reconsiderations." *DA*, 28 (1967), 637A (Wisconsin).

Sage, Judith A. "The Making of Meredith's *The Amazing Marriage*." *DA*, 28 (1968), 2222A (Ohio State).

Reade

Gettmann, R. A. "The Serialization of Reade's *A Good Fight*." *Nineteenth-Century Fiction*, 6 (1952), 21–32.

Thackeray

Bailey, John. "Thackeray and the English Novel." *Quarterly Review*, 216 (1912), 420–41.

Harden, Edgar F. "The Artistry of a Serial Novelist: Parts 10, 14, and 15 of *The Newcomes*." *Huntington Library Quarterly*, 39 (1976), 203–18.

———. "The Challenge of Serialization: Parts 4, 5, and 6 of *The Newcomes*." *Nineteenth-Century Fiction*, 29 (1974), 3–21.

———. "The Discipline and Significance of Form in *Vanity Fair*." *PMLA*, 82 (1967), 530–41.

———. *The Emergence of Thackeray's Serial Fiction*. Athens: Univ. of Georgia Press, 1979.

———. "The Growth of *The Virginians* as a Serial Novel: Parts 1–9." *Costerus*, NS 2 (1974), 217–66.

Keech, James M. " 'Make 'em Wait': Installment Suspense in Thackeray's *Vanity Fair*." *Serif*, 3 (1966), 9–12.

McCarthy, Helen L. "Thackeray and Serialization." *DA*, 22 (1961), 1612A–13A (Columbia).

Randall, David A. "Bibliographical Notes." *Papers of the Bibliographical Society of America*, 34 (1940), 191–92, 267–78.

Scarry, Elaine. "Enemy and Father: Comic Equilibrium of Number Fourteen of *Vanity Fair*." *Journal of Narrative Technique*, 10 (1980), 145–55.

Shillingsburg, Peter L. "A Date for the Early Composition of *Vanity Fair*." *English Studies*, 53 (1972), 47–52.

———. "Final Touches and Patches in *Vanity Fair*: The First Edition." *Studies in the Novel*, 13 (1981), 40–50.

———. "The First Edition of Thackeray's *Pendennis*." *Papers of the Bibliographical Society of America*, 66 (1972), 35–49.

———. "The Text of *Pendennis*." *DA*, 31 (1971), 5426A (South Carolina).

Sorensen, Gerald C. "A Critical Edition of W. M. Thackeray's *The Virginians* (Parts I–III) with *The Virginians*, Volumes I and II. London, Bradbury and Evans, 1858." *DA*, 27 (1967), 3019A (Minnesota).

Sundell, M. G. Introduction. *Twentieth Century Interpretations of* Vanity Fair: *A Collection of Critical Essays*. Ed. Sundell. Englewood Cliffs, N.J.: Prentice-Hall, 1969, pp. 1–12.

Sutherland, John A. "The Thackeray-Smith Contracts." *Studies in the Novel*, 13 (1981), 168–83.

———. *Thackeray at Work*. London: Athlone, 1974.

Trollope

D., T. C. "Victorian Editors and Victorian Delicacy." *Notes and Queries*, 187 (1944), 251–53.

Sadleir, Michael. *Trollope: A Bibliography*. London: Oxford Univ. Press, 1954.